ASSASSINS AND LIARS

THE J.R. FINN SAILING MYSTERY SERIES

C.L.R. DOUGHERTY

ASSASSINS AND LIARS

The J.R. Finn Sailing Mystery Series
Book 1

Death and Deception in the Caribbean

The Virgin Islands

Anguila

Puerto Rico

St. Martin

St. Barth

Saba

Barbuda

Statia

St. Kitts & Nevis

Antigua

Montserrat

Guadeloupe

Dominica

*Puerto Rico and
the Windward and
Leeward Islands*

Martinique

St. Lucia

St. Vincent

Bequia

The Grenadines

Grenada

Trinidad

Venezuela

St. Vincent to Carriacou

St. Vincent

Bequia

Mustique

Canouan

reefs

Mayreau

Tobago Cays

Union Island

reefs

Hillsborough

Carriacou

Petite Martinique

1

Her feet were the first things I noticed about her. That may seem strange, but it wasn't as strange as the things that happened later. Still, her feet caught my attention and that led to the rest.

About those feet. They were at eye level. That's why they were the first things I noticed. I was tying the dinghy to a cleat on the dock at the marina, and the feet stepped into my field of view. Tanned, slender, and clean. They looked cared for, but like they worked for a living. No nail polish or toe rings, just nice feet.

Oh, and the soles. She wasn't wearing shoes. Not even flip-flops. The soles of her feet were like mine. Callused, cracked, and salt-cured. Tough as leather. She went barefoot, maybe all the time. Like I said, working feet.

I finished my figure-of-eight knot and let my eyes wander up her legs. Dancer's legs, well-muscled, with smooth skin the color of *café au lait*.

The tattoo of the cobra slithering around the inside of her left thigh was lifelike, startling. It wrapped around her leg, the perspective exaggerated. With its tail hidden behind her thigh, the snake's life-sized head was heart-stopping.

It leapt from her tanned flesh; I felt myself flinch from its strike. Recovering from my shock, I overcame the urge to let my eyes linger and looked up, curious to see her face.

She had even features, no makeup. She didn't need any. Her eyes locked on mine. Gray eyes, almost colorless. They would have been cold and forbidding, except for the creases at the corners. She must smile a lot. Her face gave away nothing. She wasn't smiling now.

"Single-hander?" she asked.

"For now," I said.

"By choice? Or by chance?"

"Does it matter?" I asked.

"It might," she said. "I'd respect your privacy if it's by choice."

"And if it's by chance?" I asked.

"Then I'd offer to buy you a rum punch."

"Reckon it's my lucky day." I climbed up onto the dock.

"Mary," she said, extending her right hand.

I took it, surprised at her grip. She wasn't a slight woman, but she wasn't big enough to have a grip like that, either.

"Finn," I said, matching her grip, careful not to overdo it. I liked the way her hand felt. Solid, with enough calluses to tell me where she got the grip. Like her feet, her hands worked for their keep.

"Irish."

The way she said it made me wonder what it meant to her.

"American," I said.

"Me, too," she said, with a hint of a smile. "I meant your last name."

I nodded. She had a nice smile. "About that rum punch ... "

"Come on, then, Finn." She turned and started walking up the dock.

I skipped a step and fell in beside her, matching her pace as she headed for the tiki bar at the head of the dock. She was about my height, tall for a woman, average for a man. Our strides matched; walking with her was comfortable.

"Finn is your last name, isn't it?"

"People just call me Finn."

She nodded and kept walking. The bar was an open-air place. When I dragged a stool up for her, it woke the bartender. It was a weekday. The people who owned all the fancy sportfishing boats were in their air-conditioned offices trying to make money to pay for their boats. The real fishermen were out on the water, slaving away in the tropical sun. Things were slow in Puerto Real at best, but during the week, not much moved.

The bartender got up from his chair in the corner and shook his head, blinking, reminding me of an iguana.

"*Buenas tardes*, Finn."

"*Gracias, Julio. Y tu, también*," I said.

"*Para la senorita?*"

"Rum punch," she said, settling onto the stool and dropping her backpack on the floor.

I sat down next to her. Julio put a glass on the bar in front of her and turned to open the refrigerator. He retrieved a pitcher of rum punch and a bottle of Presidente. After he filled her glass, he pried the top off my beer and returned to his chair in the corner.

"You're a regular," she said. "You live here?"

"For now," I said. "You?"

"Passing through," she said, "looking for a boat."

She picked up her drink and extended it toward me. I clicked my beer bottle against her glass, and she took an honest swallow of the punch.

"Cheers," I said, sipping my beer. "You headed north or south?"

"It depends," she said.

"On?"

"On which way the boat's going. I mostly want out of Puerto Rico. Been here, done it. Time to move on."

She took a sip of her punch, pacing herself after that first slug. I was relieved to see that. I was interested, but not if she was a rummy.

"Where'd you come here from?" I asked.

"Miami. Deckhand on a big Perini Navi."

"Gold-plater," I said. "You cook?"

"I get by."

"Drugs?" I asked.

"You looking for a handout? Or offering to share?"

"Smart-ass," I said.

"Yep." She grinned. "Got a problem with that?"

"What if I said yes?"

"Then I'd thank you for the company and tell you to fuck off."

I laughed. I was enjoying this.

"About the drugs," she said.

I raised my eyebrows.

"I'm clean," she said. "Don't use, never did. You?"

"Same."

She nodded. "But I don't judge people. They make their own choices. Long as they don't mess me up that's okay. Everybody gets to pick their own road to hell."

I liked her. She was clean, articulate, and she was damn good looking. Not in a barfly way, either. And I liked her sense of humor.

This could work for both of us. She wanted a ride. I'd be less noticeable as half of a couple.

"You in a hurry?" I asked.

She frowned and didn't say anything.

"To leave," I said.

"Oh," she said, her face stretching into a smile like a sunrise.

I wondered what she thought I meant at first.

She shrugged. "Sooner would suit me better than later. You got a schedule or something?"

I started to tell her, then thought better of it. She probably wasn't working for them, but why risk it? I was planning to leave this evening; I only came ashore to pick up a few things at the little grocery store across the street.

"I'm itchin' for open water. Sooner's better, for sure."

"Sooner like tomorrow, maybe?"

"That could work. You really don't care where we go?"

"No, I don't. I'm tired of Puerto Rico — too big. Where are you thinking about?"

"We've got a strong northeast wind; looks like it's settled in to blow for a while. A close reach would put us in the Grenadines in four days, maybe farther north if the wind backs a little."

"All the way to the Windwards, huh?" she asked.

"It's either that or beat our brains out hammering into the wind to get to the Virgins. I'd rather spend my time on an easy sail. We could work our way back up the island chain from there if we want to."

"Sounds good," she said.

"You got a passport?" I asked.

She leaned over and picked up her backpack. Unzipping a side pouch, she extracted a dog-eared passport and handed it to me.

I looked at the mugshot; her, no doubt about that. Mary Elizabeth O'Brien. Twenty-four years old. I flipped through it — not many stamps, given the rough shape it was in. I gave it back, and she zipped it away, lowering the backpack to the floor again.

"Want to go sailing for a while?" I asked.

"Sure," she said. "I'm game."

"Should we go get your stuff?"

She gave me a hard look. "There's something we need to talk about, first."

I raised my eyebrows, inviting her to continue.

"I'm a woman," she said, and paused.

I nodded. "I guessed that."

"And you're not."

"Not last time I checked, anyhow."

"There's this thing men and women do. Sex."

I held her gaze and said nothing.

"It could happen," she said, "or not. I'm not narrow-minded, but I'm not easy. If it happens because both of us want it, that's okay. If you think it's how I'm paying my way, get over it."

I nodded. "I'm with you. If it happens, it happens. Or not. We'll just have to see." I was a little surprised that she seemed to take my word for that. Either desperate or naïve, I figured. I was wrong, I was soon to learn. About the naïveté, at least.

"Let's go see this fine vessel of yours," she said, standing up. She pulled a rumpled bill from her pocket and put it under her half-full glass of punch.

I took a last swig of beer and got up. "Where's your stuff?"

She hefted the backpack and turned. "I travel light," she said, leading the way back to the dinghy dock.

2

"LET'S GO GET THOSE GROCERIES," MARY SAID.

"Now?" I asked. We'd only been aboard *Island Girl* for about ten minutes. In that short time, she stowed her backpack in the empty locker I showed her and went back on deck.

She checked the tension of the shrouds, putting her weight into it, and cast a critical eye over the rest of the rig. Back below deck, she opened lockers and exercised the through-hull fittings, yanking hard on the hoses attached to them. She was no novice; I saw her eyes narrow at a few things that could use attention.

When I thought she was finished, she pulled the scrap of indoor/outdoor carpet up from the cabin sole and lifted the panel that exposed the bilge sump. She stuck her head in the bilge and took a deep breath. Putting the panel and the carpet back in place, she stood up.

"Well?" I asked.

"She'll do," she said, moving on to the galley, opening drawers and lockers one by one.

I was licking my wounded pride; this was my home she was

talking about. "She'll do?" I asked, trying to keep the emotion out of my voice.

She looked at me for a long few seconds and said. "Yeah, she'll do. She's no beauty, but she's ready. She'll take us wherever we want to go."

I just nodded, not trusting myself to say anything.

"What do you need from the grocery store?" she asked.

"Peanut butter, a couple of loaves of bread. Some snack food, depending on what they've got."

"That's it?" she asked.

"Yeah, unless you want something."

"You're fond of beans and rice," she said. "Looks like a lifetime supply, and you have plenty of smoked *chorizo* to go with 'em."

"You don't like my diet?" I asked. "What more do you want?"

"I love beans and rice with *chorizo*," she said. "But we need tomatoes and fresh onions. A couple of heads of garlic, too."

"What for?"

"Beans and rice are good for you. Throw in a few extras, and it makes 'em taste like they're worth eating. The *chorizo's* a good start, but the other stuff makes a big difference. You okay with that?"

"Sure. I'm pretty easy when it comes to food; it's just fuel."

"Yeah," she said. "Life's short. Might as well eat fuel that tastes good."

"There's a big grocery store about a ten-minute walk east of town," I said.

"No need," she said. "Not unless you want something else. The little place across the street will have everything we need. Let's go now; I'll cook supper when we get back. We can make an early evening of it if you still want to get out of here in the morning."

"Let's go," I said.

She climbed back up into the cockpit and pulled the dinghy

alongside. I untied the painter and held it while she got settled in the little inflatable. I lowered myself into it and started the outboard, heading back to the dinghy dock.

When we got there, she tied the dinghy up and locked it as if she did it every day. That dock was maybe five feet above the water. This is where I came face to feet with her not long ago. I was trying to wriggle by her so I could clamber up and give her a hand. Then she stood up, facing away from me. She was right in front of me, blocking my way.

She put her right hand on the dock, gave a little jump, and vaulted up. I was pretty sure no part of her body touched the dock except the palm of her one hand and the soles of her feet. Damnedest thing I'd ever seen, like a gymnast or something. Next thing I knew, I was standing there in the dinghy admiring those feet again.

I took a deep breath and hoped I could get up there without embarrassing myself. Fortunately, she turned away, so she didn't see me struggling. But I think she guessed. Once I was standing next to her, she looked around at me and smiled.

"You okay?" she asked.

I gave her one of my taciturn nods, and she started walking up the dock. I skipped a step or two and caught up with her, matching her pace again. Damn, I liked walking next to her. "You're pretty fit," I said.

"I work out. You?"

"Well, I swim a lot."

"That's good for you," she said.

By then, we were walking out the marina gate. I've spent a good bit of my forty years in hostile environments. Situational awareness is deeply engrained in me; that's why I'm still walking around. I saw the car idling at the curb on the opposite side of the street and thought it looked out of place. There was a guy behind the wheel and two in the back seat.

With practiced speed, the two passengers jumped out, both

on the street side, leaving the door open. One grabbed Mary, and the other took a swing at me. I slipped his punch, hooked his ankle, and gave him a shove on the back of his shoulder. His momentum took him to the ground. The other one held Mary in a bear hug, dragging her toward the car.

I knew the drill; if they got her in the car, it was over, whatever *it* was. I rushed the car. The driver's window was open. He was shifting his eyes from the rearview mirror to the windshield, watching for traffic.

He saw me, but it was too late for him to react. I hit him below his left ear with my right fist, all of my 185 pounds behind it. He flew across the front seat and landed in a pile against the passenger door. I snatched the keys from the ignition and dropped them in my pocket.

I turned, ready to go back and deal with the two who were grappling with Mary. Before I took more than a couple of steps, I watched her go limp in the bear hug. The guy holding her staggered forward, her dead weight throwing him off balance.

The other one was getting back on his feet. He took one step toward Mary and she dug both heels into the pavement and lurched back, legs pumping like mad. She drove the guy holding her back against the wall of the building. He came to a bone-jarring stop against the concrete.

Mary snapped her head back, smashing the back of her skull into his nose with an audible crunch. He let her go, but not before she raised her right foot behind her and raked it down the front of his right leg. She caught her foot on the top edge of his kneecap and put her weight on it. All that happened in the time I took to get to the other man, who was still closing on Mary.

The one whose knee she dislocated started screaming and fell to the sidewalk. Mary squatted and pivoted on her left foot, coming up with her right foot snapping out at head height. Her heel connected with the point of the last man's chin just as I grabbed him from behind. I heard the crack of his jawbone breaking as the force of her strike knocked us both down.

"Good move on the car," she said, as I slithered out from under her unconscious victim.

"I've seen this play before," I said. "As long as they didn't drive away with you, I figured we'd be good."

I got to my feet in time to see her spin and plant another one of her deadly kicks on the side of her first assailant's head. That's when I realized he was screaming non-stop, when she knocked him into oblivion and it got dead quiet.

"About the groceries," I said.

She grinned. "Beans and rice with just *chorizo* can taste pretty good when you're hungry," she said. "I think we should haul ass. Somebody's probably called the cops, after all the racket this crybaby made."

"Walk back to the dinghy fast, but don't run," I said. "Be cool."

"Got it, skipper. It's not my first time, either."

3

"CAN'T YOU MAKE THIS THING GO ANY FASTER?" MARY ASKED.

We were halfway back to *Island Girl* when we heard the first sirens.

"Nope. This is all she'll do. Soon as we're alongside, let me get aboard and fire up the diesel. While I'm doing that, you take the outboard off the transom and hand it to me. With me so far?"

"Yes."

"Once we've got the outboard off, climb up with the painter and the stern line. Give me the stern line and we'll swing the dinghy up on deck. While I get the anchor in, you let the air out of the dinghy and roll it up. Get it lashed down on deck as best you can."

"Got it, Finn," she said, as I killed the outboard and scrambled over the lifelines.

I got the diesel running and turned around to find the outboard resting on the side deck. Mary stood next to it, holding the stern line out for me. I took it, and we lifted the empty inflatable aboard. She bent to open the three air valves.

The air hissed out while I picked up the little outboard and clamped it on the stern rail where I stored it.

The dinghy was half-flat by the time I pulled the anchor in and lashed it in its chocks. I stepped behind the helm and got *Island Girl* under way. Mary was rolling the inflatable, forcing the remaining air out. She lashed it down in front of the mast by the time I negotiated the dog-leg in the channel.

I could still hear the sirens in the distance. We would be gone from the harbor by the time the cops got to town.

"I forgot to say thanks," Mary said, joining me in the cockpit.

"You're welcome," I said. "It was kind of hectic back there."

"If you're okay for a few minutes, I'll go below and cook dinner. You're headed for Cabo Rojo, right?"

"Yeah."

"I should be able to get it done by the time we get there. It'll be too rough to cook once we round the cape."

"Use the pressure cooker," I said. "It's — "

"I saw it," she said, backing down the companionway ladder.

She was still working in the galley when I left the harbor entrance channel. There wasn't much breeze; the island was blocking the trade winds. We would find cape-effect wind as we approached Cabo Rojo. It would be blowing right from the direction we wanted to go.

I planned to motor along close to shore to avoid the foul wind as long as I could. That meant burning diesel fuel, but the tank was full. Once we cleared the cape, we could make sail.

I was itching to ask her about the three guys in the car, but I knew she wouldn't be able to hear me over the engine noise. The engine box is right next to the galley. I'd just have to be patient.

She was right about the rough water to come. Once we hit Cabo Rojo, we'd have ten or twelve hours before things settled down enough for us to enjoy the ride again.

Thinking of the three thugs reminded me that I snatched their car keys. I fished them from my pocket and saw a rental company's tag on them. I could check on who rented the car, if need be. Mary might know who they were, but would she share that with me?

When she first invited herself to come along, I figured she would be company on a long voyage and give me a little camouflage, in the bargain.

If the people I was going to see were watching for me, which was a safe bet, they wouldn't be expecting me in my current, weather-beaten incarnation. Certainly, they wouldn't expect me to have an attractive young woman in tow.

Now, though, I was wondering what kind of baggage that attractive young woman carried besides her backpack. Three guys in a rental car trying to kidnap her wasn't exactly traveling light, to my way of thinking.

Chances were those boys weren't trying to snatch a woman at random. First, they were too well organized. Second, they sure as hell wouldn't have staked out the marina in Puerto Real, not on a weekday afternoon. Puerto Real's a quiet little fishing village, except for weekend sport fishermen.

If I guessed right, those three were looking for Mary in particular. That meant somebody would eventually get around to asking Julio, the bartender, about her. They saw us come from the marina, and Julio was an obvious source of information, tucked back in his corner of the bar.

I was just rolling all that around in my mind when she set two steaming bowls of black beans and rice on the bridge deck. She scrambled up the companionway ladder and stood up, watching my reaction as I took in the bikini she was almost wearing.

I've got a decent poker face, but it must have failed me, because she laughed at me. A nice, musical laugh, that made me want to tell her all the jokes I knew, just so I could hear more of it.

I shook my head and shifted my position, draping my left leg over the tiller to hold our course. As I reached toward the bowls, she dropped to the seat across from me and picked one up, handing it to me.

"It was hot down in the galley," she said. "I'll get dressed in a minute, as soon as I cool off."

"Take your time," I said. "Might as well be comfortable."

She laughed again and leaned forward, reaching for the other bowl. I knew there was something I needed to ask her, but I couldn't for the life of me remember what it was.

4

"WAITING TO MAKE SAIL UNTIL WE ROUND THE CAPE?" SHE ASKED.

"Yep," I answered, between mouthfuls. "Good job on dinner. You put something in here besides the *chorizo*, didn't you?"

"Yes. I have a few packets of *sazón* in my backpack. You like it okay?"

"Better than okay," I said, resisting the urge to lick my empty bowl. "But that seems like a funny thing to have in your backpack."

She smiled, but she didn't offer an explanation. I didn't press her. Of all the odd things she could have in the backpack, seasoning mix wasn't high on my list of worries. She finished her dinner and picked my bowl up.

"More?" she asked. "There's plenty. I figured we could warm it up later instead of having to cook again."

"Good for you. You've done this before."

"I told you I had." She was frowning.

"I meant sailing a small boat in open water. You told me about crewing on a Perini Navi. What was it? Hundred thirty feet?"

"Give or take," she said. "Why?"

"No reason. It's just a little different offshore on a 34-footer. Things like cooking, for example."

"Oh," she said. "Yeah, that's true. I grew up in a sailing family. Thirty-four feet's big compared to what I learned on. My father raced Lightnings."

"You wouldn't have done much cooking on a Lightning."

She chuckled. "No. My brother's got an old Folkboat. The two of us did a little cruising on that when I was in college."

I nodded.

"If you're done eating," she said, "I'll go wash these up and square away the galley. Should I make a thermos of coffee for the evening watch?"

"Sure. The thermos is — "

"I saw it," she said, standing up with a bowl in each hand. "In the locker with the coffee pot and the coffee. Let me go get everything taken care of before it gets rough, okay?"

"Sure. I was enjoying the company."

She gave me another one of those smiles that took my breath away. "Me, too. We'll talk more."

She went below, and I was alone with the rumble of the diesel.

When she came back, I planned to raise the topic of the three men who tried to get her in the car in Puerto Real. I thought she might bring it up herself. There was plenty of opportunity, but she kept the conversation to sailing and food.

And that took me back to my thoughts before she served our dinner. When somebody got around to following up on what happened to the three men, they would find Julio, the bartender at the place in the marina.

A little time would pass before that happened, though. Those men would be tangled up with the cops for a while, and the two who mixed it up with Mary would spend some hospital time recovering.

Once somebody found Julio, he would take their money

and answer their questions. But he didn't know much about the gringo named Finn.

He could tell them I drank Presidente and tipped well. I lived on a beat-up little sloop named *Island Girl*. The boat was in the harbor for a week. And that was all Julio knew about me.

I didn't tell anybody where I came from or where I was going. There were a few boat names that were more common than *Island Girl*, but not many. They'd have a tough time following us, unless they could track Mary somehow.

That was why I needed to get her to tell me what was going on in her life. Puerto Rico's not huge, but there are lots of boats there. Most of the yachts in transit were on the other end of the island.

The boats in Puerto Real stayed there for the long term. Not many visitors pass through, like I did. Mary's story of trying to hitch a ride didn't ring true.

Something caused the three men to look for her in Puerto Real. The worst case would be that somebody planted a tracking device in Mary's stuff. That could cause a problem for us.

And I wanted to know what brought her to Puerto Real. Like I said, it wasn't high on the list of places to hitch a ride on a cruising boat. *Island Girl* was the only cruising boat there during my stay.

That brought me to one more niggling little worry. I wondered about the bikini. After my initial shock, I ignored that as best I could. It *was* hot below, especially when you were cooking. Or was she trying to distract me?

It almost worked; she was an eyeful, but I've been around the block too many times to fall prey to that trick. Besides, she was twenty-four. She was only about six years older than my — No. I'm not going to do that. Mary's enough of a distraction until I figure out what her game is.

At least I got a better look at that cobra tattooed on her

thigh. When I first saw it, the head just below the denim of her cutoffs, I didn't take in much but the head, with its gaping mouth and dripping fangs.

Thanks to the bikini and her moving around the cockpit, I had a better appreciation for the skill of the artist. The snake's tail wrapped around her upper thigh, tapering into a coil down close to the back of her knee.

When she came up into the cockpit to pick up the dishes of beans and rice, her back was to me. As she turned to hand me the dish, my eyes involuntarily followed the cobra's body around her thigh. The ripple of her muscles beneath her skin and the perspective of the art brought the cobra to life. I flinched as I came face to face with it, just like I did the first time.

The tail on the back of her thigh seemed too small to belong to the snake on the front. That added to the shock effect when she turned; the tattoo was meant to frighten. As amazing as the artwork was, something about that snake still didn't quite add up.

The tattoo was threatening, especially after seeing her destroy those two thugs. Otherwise, she gave the impression of a clean-cut young woman.

Why would she have such an out-of-character tattoo? Young women had tattoos these days, but not like that. What did that say about her? Was she...

"Shit, Finn. Stop it," I mumbled to myself.

"You say something?" she asked, peering out of the companionway.

"Just clearing my throat," I said.

"You want coffee now?" she asked.

"No. I'll save it until I need it tonight. You done with the dishes?"

"Yes." She climbed into the cockpit, one arm cradling the thermos. "Is there somewhere to stash this up here?"

"Stick it in that storage netting on the starboard side of the footwell." I noticed she put the T-shirt and cutoffs back on. Maybe she *did* just get hot working over the stove earlier.

"What about watches?" she asked, plopping down on the seat across from me.

"I'm flexible," I said. "I'm used to being solo, so any help will be a luxury. Do you have any preference?"

"How about four hours on, four off?" she asked.

"Sounds good to me if it'll work for you."

"I'm pretty wired right now," she said. "I would say I'd take her and let you get some rest, but it'll be dark soon. Maybe you should get us around Cabo Rojo and in open water before I take her. Strange boat, and all."

"That's fine. I'm wired, too. Besides, it'll be easier to get the sails up with both of us on deck. We should round the cape in another hour. Then we'll see how things are going."

"Okay," she said. "About the elephant in the room ..."

"I thought maybe you hadn't noticed," I said.

"I knew it was there. I just wasn't ready to talk about it. Thanks for not pressing me."

"You're welcome, but I gotta tell you, my curiosity was about to get the best of me. I figured you'd tell me about it when you were ready, or when I couldn't stand to wait any longer."

"You're a strange man, Finn. In a nice way, I mean."

"Thanks, I guess."

She gave me another one of those smiles. "You're welcome. It was a compliment. You're comfortable to be with. But about those three men ..."

"Yes? Who were they?" I asked.

"I don't know. They've been watching me since I got off the Perini Navi in Fajardo. They spooked me; I'll tell you that."

"Watching you? Any idea why?"

She shook her head. "It was weird, like I'd glimpse one of them out of the corner of my eye every so often. That was at first. Then I realized it was two different men. And everywhere I went, one or the other of them would pop up." She shuddered.

"You'd never seen them before that?"

She shook her head. "No."

"Can you connect them with the yacht? The Perini Navi?"

"No."

"Did it have a name?"

"*Sisyphus*," she said. "You know the reference?"

"The son of Aeolus," I said. "Condemned to roll that rock up the hill over and over forever. I've had days like that."

"Me, too."

"Who owns her?"

"I don't know. None of the crew did. Well, I guess maybe the captain did. But nobody made the trip out except crew. No guests."

"Were you paid crew?"

"I was supposed to be. They stiffed me, but that's another story."

"We've got time."

She pursed her lips and looked away for several seconds, watching the sun sinking toward the horizon.

"There were a dozen people in the crew — nine men and three women. The women were stewardesses, except for me. I was a deckhand. The mate and the rest of the guys, they passed the women around. The captain wasn't part of it, but he didn't do anything to stop it, either. It was like part of the job, one of the stewardesses told me. 'Go along to get along,' she said. Not my style."

"So, they booted you without paying you?"

"Well, there's a little more to it. The mate was abusive when I wouldn't play along with him. I kind of broke his arm."

"Kind of?" I chuckled at that.

"Yeah. In two places. And a few of his ribs. He was a wimp; ended up spending the rest of the voyage laid up in his cabin taking pain pills. So they didn't pay me. Captain threatened to press charges if I made trouble about it. Like that."

"Uh-huh," I said. "Where'd you learn to handle yourself, anyway? You made short work of those guys in Puerto Real. Did a lot of damage in a hurry."

"My brother."

"The one with the boat?"

"Right."

"He some kind of badass?"

"He was. He was into mixed martial arts, a cage fighter. Never lost a match. Until ..." She shook her head.

"Did something happen to him?"

"He was in the National Guard. He was wounded in Iraq and discharged with a disability pension."

"Ouch," I said. "I guess his mixed martial arts days are over."

"Yes and no. He could still fight, but they won't let him. He lost his temper in a couple of matches. He was about to kill one guy; they stopped the match. It took three people to pull him off the other fighter."

"Back to those three guys in the car," I said. "You think maybe they were friends of the mate on *Sisyphus*?"

She shrugged. "I don't know, but if they were, why were they following me? They could have jumped me anywhere. Why in Puerto Real?"

Good point, I thought. "What were you doing in Puerto Real?"

"I couldn't get another paid crew position. The people on *Sisyphus* blacklisted me with the crew agencies. I looked for volunteer crew jobs, but I guess it's the wrong time of the year, or something. And most of the private boats were sailed by couples or families. They weren't looking for crew. I ran across a few single-handers, but there was a reason they were single-handers, you know? Anyhow, I decided to see a little of Puerto

Rico while I was there. I was working my way around the island, and Puerto Real was on my route."

"You think maybe those guys were following you to make sure you didn't leave the island?"

"I didn't think of that. You're saying when they saw me connect with you they decided to stop me? But why?"

"I don't have any answers, Mary. It was just a thought."

"You okay for a little while?" she asked.

"Sure. Why?"

"I need to use the head, and it's almost time to make sail. I'll be back in a few minutes."

5

By the time Mary came back on deck, we were within a mile of Cabo Rojo. The easterly trade wind was whipping around the cape, blowing right in our faces.

"Might as well make sail," I said. "We'll put her on a close reach on the port tack and ride the wind around the cape. Once we're well clear, it should have backed enough for us to lay a southeasterly course. What do you think?"

"Makes sense," she said. "What would you like for me to do? Hoist the main, or take the helm?"

"Sea state's sloppy," I said. "I'll uncover the main and raise it; I know all the boat's little peculiarities. Time enough for you to learn her quirks when it's not so rough."

"You're the skipper," she said, settling onto the cockpit seat across from me and reaching for the tiller. "I'll wait until you've got the cover off the main before I head her up into the wind."

"Good enough," I said, rising to a crouch and opening the locker under my seat. I took out two safety harnesses with tethers attached. Handing her one, I slipped mine on and snapped it closed. She watched as I re-hooked the tether, making sure the carabiner passed through both of the D-rings on the belt.

"I'll take the tiller while you get the harness on and get it adjusted," I said.

She nodded and slipped her arms through the harness, fastening the belt under her ribcage and pulling it tight. "Harnesses all the time?" she asked.

I nodded. "Any time you're on deck. Hook the tether to that eye bolt down in the footwell while you're in the cockpit. There's another tether hooked on each jackline — one on each side of the coachroof. If you're going out of the cockpit, hook up to a jackline before you unhook the tether to the eyebolt, okay?"

"Got it," she said. "Don't worry; I'm a true believer."

"Good for you. It's amazing how many people aren't."

"Yeah. There are lots of fools running loose. Don't they see it's a death sentence to go overboard offshore?" she asked, readjusting the harness.

"Guess not."

I waited until she was hooked up and comfortable with the fit of her harness. She took the tiller again, and I hooked on to the port jackline and climbed onto the coachroof, crabbing my way to the base of the mast.

The fiberglass was wet with wind-driven spray, and slick in the spots that didn't have non-skid. I faced Mary and wrapped my left arm over the covered main. Working my way aft, I undid the common-sense fasteners along the underside of the boom as I went.

When I reached the end of the boom, I turned around, switched arms, and folded the sail cover, rolling it along the boom as I went back to the mast. I untied the sail ties as I came to them, stuffing them in my waistband. Once at the mast, I undid the fasteners holding the cover along the front of the mast and tied the bundled sail cover to the base of the mast.

I unhooked the main halyard from the eye at the base of the

mast. Shackling it to the headboard of the mainsail with my right hand, I held on with my left as *Island Girl* smashed into the building waves. The swell that wrapped around Cabo Rojo was giving us a rough ride. I freed the halyard from the cleat near its winch and pulled in the slack. Taking the winch handle from its holder, I snapped it into the winch.

I turned my head and looked back at Mary. She nodded and held up the tail of the mainsheet, letting me know it was running free. I nodded back, and she pushed the tiller to the port. That brought the bow dead into the wind. I hoisted the mainsail hand over hand, keeping my head down to avoid the flogging canvas and the swinging boom.

When I couldn't gain any more on the halyard, I put my right hand on the winch handle and cranked a couple of turns, tailing with my left hand. I cleated the halyard and turned to Mary, giving her a wave. She turned the bow about 30 degrees to the west and hauled in on the mainsheet, her foot on the tiller to hold our course.

The sail filled with an audible crack. *Island Girl* liked that. She heeled over to the starboard, almost putting her rail in the water. Her erratic motion settled, giving way to an easy surge. The lift from the sail carried her smoothly over the waves that were now striking us at about a 45-degree angle to the bow of the boat.

I grinned when I saw Mary bend to the engine instrument panel and pull the shutdown knob. She knew what she was doing. Looking up at me, she gave me one of those smiles and raised a thumb and her eyebrows, then she extended her index finger, pointing at the headstay. She was asking if I wanted to raise the jib. I gave her a nod and went forward.

Two minutes later, I sat down in the cockpit across from her and glanced at the knot meter. We were making five knots on a close reach under a full main and a 100-percent jib. The ride was nice; *Island Girl* was in her element rolling smoothly over the waves.

"Good job," I said. "Thanks; we'll make a good team."

"I think so," she said. "You normally do that all alone?"

"Sure. You get used to it. I put a piece of bungee cord on the tiller and throttle way back, just enough power to keep her bow into the wind. Then I raise the sails and let 'em flog until I get back to the cockpit. But it was nice to have your help. You know your stuff."

She nodded, taking my compliment in stride. "Ever wish you had roller furling on the headstay?"

"No. It's unnecessary on a boat this size, and it's dangerous."

"The new ones are more reliable," she said. "Or so I hear."

"You've done enough of this to know things only fail at the worst possible moment," I said. "I've seen those oversized boats with a husband and wife crew come limping in with shredded jibs because the bearings in the furler froze in a squall. Besides, I like being able to fly different sized jibs to match the wind and the sea state."

"Amen," she said.

We sailed along in comfortable silence, watching the course creeping around to the southeast as Mary followed the wind around Cabo Rojo. By the time we were clear of the cape, the wind was blowing a steady 15 knots from the east-northeast. We were holding a course of about 130 degrees magnetic.

"I've got her," Mary said, after several minutes. "Why don't I take the first watch and let you rest?"

"I'm still wired up, but thanks. I'm used to this, remember? I don't really relax until I'm out of sight of land."

She nodded and didn't say anything. I liked that. She was a good shipmate. After five or ten minutes, she said, "You don't mind the company, do you? I'll go below if you'd rather have your solitude."

I smiled at her and shook my head. "It's nice to share this with you. There'll be plenty of time for solitude."

"You want to talk? Or just enjoy the sunset?" she asked.

"Both," I said. "But thanks for asking."

"I know how nice it is to be alone on watch, sometimes," she said.

I nodded. "But it's nice to share a watch with a comfortable shipmate, every so often."

"Why, thank you, Finn. I think that was a compliment."

"Yes," I said "It was. And you're welcome. It's nice to have you aboard. Looks like we'll have a good trip to wherever."

"We've settled in on about 130 to 140 degrees, now," she said. "Where's that going to take us?"

"Somewhere between St. Lucia and St. Vincent, I'd say. We could end up farther south, depending on how the wind holds."

"That okay with you? Or should we trim the sails?"

"It's fine with me for now. We'll keep an eye on it over the next few days. You okay with it?"

"Sure. I'm just along for the ride."

"No destination, no schedule?" I asked.

"That's my plan, and I'm sticking to it," she said, smacking a fist on the cockpit seat.

I laughed. "I like you, Mary Elizabeth O'Brien."

She smiled. "Thanks, just Finn."

"My pleasure," I said.

After a few minutes listening to sounds of the boat, she said, "My family and close friends call me Mary Beth."

"That an invitation?"

"If you'd like. Looks like we're going to be close friends for a while, anyhow."

"Good. I like that. Mary Beth suits you." I waited, thinking she would ask what my friends called me, wondering how to answer her. But she didn't ask.

We passed an hour in easy silence, and when the sun was

fully down, I said, "Excuse me; I'd better go turn on the nav lights and mark our position. You want anything when I come back on deck?"

"No, thanks. But you don't have to come back up if you feel like a nap. I like your company, but I can take a watch now, if you'd like."

How could I pass that up? I liked her company, too. I could sleep later. I switched on the nav lights and wrote our position in the log, along with our course and speed, and the date and time. I went back up to the cockpit and we sailed along in moonlit silence, each alone with our thoughts.

Feeling her hand on my shoulder, I jerked upright and opened my eyes, looking around, alarmed and confused.

"It's okay," she said. "You've been asleep about four hours. Everything's fine; course and speed are the same. You good?"

"Yes, fine," I said. "Sorry I was such boring company."

She gave me that smile of hers and said, "You needed the rest. Pour yourself some coffee, and then I'm going below and stretch out for a while."

I nodded and filled a coffee cup. "The starboard settee's the best sea berth," I said. "There's a lee cloth under the cushions. Pull it out and snap the hooks to the pad eyes overhead."

"Okay. Thanks. Call me if you need me," she said, leaning over and brushing her lips against my whiskers. Then she smiled and disappeared into the gloom below, leaving me thinking I'd better shave soon.

6

I watched Mary Beth set up the lee cloth and crawl into the berth. She blew me a kiss and turned off the dim red night light, leaving me alone with my thoughts. I found myself stroking the spot on my cheek where she kissed me a few minutes earlier. I pulled my hand away, embarrassed. Did she see that?

Surely it was my imagination, but the spot felt warm. I shook my head. My interactions with women since my divorce 20-odd years ago were catch-as-catch-can. I was out of practice at dealing with flirtatious women, especially young, pretty ones.

What the hell were you thinking, Finn? You're committed to a mission; you have to be in St. Vincent in five days, and you can't have this girl tagging along when you execute. How did you get sucked into this?

My rationale that she was camouflage was just an excuse for falling prey to her hustle. She could be camouflage, but only if I were willing to let her get killed — or kill her myself — to cover my tracks. And neither option set well with me. Frustrated with myself, I acknowledged that I felt the need to protect her. *Why, you old fool? She may only be a few years older than your daughter, but she's hardly an innocent child. And how did she end up in Puerto Real just in time to hitch a ride with you, anyway?*

I thought back to when I saw her at the dinghy dock. I was focused on picking up the stuff I needed at the grocery store and getting underway. I wasn't in a bind from a schedule standpoint, but I didn't have time to waste, either. My target was expected to leave St. Vincent for Europe soon. I could deal with him in Europe, but St. Vincent was a far better spot for an execution.

Mary Beth looked good standing on that dinghy dock, and I was feeling lonely, and maybe a little too comfortable for my own good. This was my second mission since I 'retired' from active service with the arcane government organization that employed me for the past 20 years.

My time with them and my previous active duty time with the Army qualified me for a nice pension with benefits. When they offered me the option of contract work after I retired, I thought it would be an occasional thing. So far though, I might as well still be active. Two missions in two months — that was more work than I was accustomed to before I retired. The money was far better, now, though. And I did have some leeway when it came to accepting assignments.

Plus, now that I was a contractor, I could choose how I carried out my missions. If I wanted to take company along with me, I was free to do that — at my own expense, of course. Mary Beth wasn't a problem to my client, as I called them now, but she might be a problem to me.

I didn't know the first thing about her, except that she was pretty, and she was sending signals that she found me attractive. I'm not normally impulsive, and I never fell for a honey trap before. Could Mary Beth be part of a setup?

I chewed the inside of my cheek as I let that possibility roll around in my mind. She was in the right place at the right time, and she pushed buttons I didn't know I had. She also kicked ass when those three goons tried to snatch her.

That added a couple of dimensions to the problem. The first was how she came to be so good at hand-to-hand combat; the second was what was going on with those three men. Her explanations were marginally adequate.

She could have learned her skills from a brother who was a cage fighter, but the way she handled herself showed more than just basic know-how. Her speed and agility argued that she got regular practice.

Her story about the men following her around Puerto Rico was strange, too. She implied that they were somehow connected to her problems aboard *Sisyphus*, but if so, there was something more to that story.

If she were part of a setup, who could be behind it, and why? There were only two reasons somebody might want to capture me. And if I were the target, what happened in Puerto Real was meant to be a snatch, not a hit. Those guys weren't trying to kill either of us, but it was possible I was their intended victim and Mary Beth was bait to lure me into their clutches.

There were people who might want to pick my brain, if they understood who I was and what I did for a living. I knew where 20 years' worth of bodies were buried, literally. There was enough information in my head to cause the U.S. government some serious embarrassment. To someone with that goal, I was only valuable if taken alive.

The other possibility was that whoever was backing my current target wanted to take me out to protect him. That was a less likely explanation. First, they would have tried to kill me, and they didn't. Second, that would mean there was a leak from the government department I worked for. That was possible, but not likely. It was a tiny organization, well-hidden in the

Department of Defense, and in my 20 years with them, there was never even a hint of a leak.

Then again, this could all be about Mary Beth, and her encounter with me could have been pure chance. I was a lonely middle-aged guy, and she was an attractive young woman. But even if that were the case, there was still more to her story than she'd told me. I resolved to work on that over the next few days.

7

"Hey, Finn," Mary said, poking her head up through the companionway as the first hint of dawn broke on the eastern horizon.

"Is it time already?" I asked.

"Four hours." She rubbed her eyes and climbed up a step or two, turning to face the bow, looking at the beginnings of the sunrise. She braced her thigh on the edge of the opening and stretched her arms over her head.

The T-shirt she slept in rode up; she wore nothing under it. I swallowed hard and averted my gaze, but not before I noticed another small tattoo centered on the untanned skin of her left hip. I didn't get a good enough look to tell what it was, and I wasn't about to stare.

"Sorry!" she said, tugging the hem of the shirt down as she turned to face me. "I forgot." She giggled and stepped into the cockpit.

"Forgot what?" I asked, keeping my eyes locked on the compass.

"Oh, nothing." She plopped down on the seat right next to

me, her hip against mine. "It's always chilly at sea this time of day."

I nodded and wrapped an arm around her shoulders, glancing over at her. She squeezed herself up against me and gave me a kiss on the cheek.

"Beautiful morning," she said. "Give me a second to get my bearings and I'll go make us some breakfast."

"Take your time." I was enjoying the way she felt, snuggled under my arm, her head on my shoulder. "Did you rest well?"

"Slept like a baby. The seas have laid down, haven't they?"

"Yes. We're well offshore. There's a long-period, four-foot easterly swell running, with a little trade wind chop. Perfect sailing."

"Did you have a good watch?" she asked.

"I did. No complaints from me."

"I saw there were some eggs in the fridge. Scrambled sound good?" she asked.

"Yes, and toast to go with them, but why don't you enjoy the sunrise first?"

"You sure you don't want to eat and crash?"

"I'm okay. I'll hang out with you up here for a little while after we eat, then take a nap. Not sure I need a full four hours of sleep. I dozed a little, I'm afraid."

"Single-hander's habit?"

"Yes. I set the alarm on my watch to go off every fifteen minutes, so I can scan the horizon for traffic. That way I can't sleep long enough to get in trouble. I didn't see another boat the whole time. There's not much going on out here; we're pretty far off the beaten path."

"Mm." She turned her head, watching the first hint of the sun peek over the horizon. "Nice." She wriggled a little, adjusting her position against my side as we watched the sunrise.

Once the show was over, she sat up. "Okay. Scrambled eggs

and toast with coffee, coming right up." She went below and began making cooking noises in the galley.

A few minutes later, she set two plates of eggs and toast on the bridge deck, followed in a moment by two steaming mugs of coffee and the thermos. She joined me in the cockpit and handed me my plate.

I noticed with relief that she was wearing her cutoffs; maybe she did just forget earlier. As attractive as she looked, I wasn't ready to add a new level of complexity to our relationship just yet.

I was hungry; I made quick work of the eggs and toast. She smiled and handed me a mug of coffee.

"More eggs?" she asked.

I grinned. "No, thanks. But that was a treat. I'm not used to having someone cook my breakfast." I took a sip of coffee.

"Glad you enjoyed it. It's the least I can do; I really appreciate your hospitality."

"My pleasure. I'm happy to have the company and the help. You're good crew."

"I hope so. I was thinking last night when I went to sleep that you took a big chance letting me tag along."

"No more of a chance than you took. Hitching rides on boats with strangers is pretty risky."

She smiled. "I'm a good judge of people; you look like the kind of man a girl can trust. I've had some experience with that kind of thing."

"Speaking of that, I don't mean to pry, but tell me a little about Mary Beth O'Brien, if you don't mind."

"Fair enough. I don't mind, but I'm not sure where to start. Give me a clue?"

"How did you end up crewing on superyachts, for starters?"

She nodded and raised her coffee mug to her lips. "I finished college a little over a year ago, but I wasn't ready to settle down and go to work. I came into a little money before I graduated, so I decided to do some traveling."

"And your family was okay with that?"

"Well, yes. I don't have much close family left, unfortunately. My parents died during my last year at school."

"I'm sorry to hear that. Just your brother, then?"

"Right. And we aren't that close. There's too big an age difference, I guess. Anyhow, I spent a year kicking around, sightseeing. Europe for a while, a little time in Asia. Then Australia and New Zealand."

"Wow. You've covered some ground. Which country do you like best?"

"They all have something to recommend them, but overall, there's no place like home, you know?"

"The good ol' U.S. of A., huh?"

"Yes. But I wanted to see the Caribbean, and I figured the best way to do it was working my way on a yacht."

"Was *Sisyphus* your first berth?"

"Yes. I had no clue. Aside from having to deal with the abusive men, being a deck hand is hard work. There's always something to scrub or scrape or paint. Polish the metal, wipe down the brightwork and touch up the varnish. Like I said, I had no idea."

"Boat maintenance is endless, all right. And the workload increases exponentially with the size of the boat. *Island Girl* is plenty big enough for me to take care of."

"She's a nice boat," Mary Beth said. "Nothing fancy, but she's solid and comfortable. Have you always sailed by yourself?"

"Mostly. I haven't been doing this full-time for all that long."

"What did you do before? If you don't mind my asking."

"I retired a year or so ago."

"Military?"

"Why do you ask?"

She shrugged. "You have that air about you. Like my brother and his friends."

I nodded. "Army. I was commissioned when I graduated from college."

"Where did you go to school?"

"University of Florida. You?"

"USF," she said. "I majored in accounting, because that's what my father wanted me to do. I was supposed to join the family business, but it wasn't to be. And I hated accounting. What did you study?"

"Engineering, but I never really worked at it. And after 20 years, my pension's enough to keep me afloat."

"Ha, afloat, huh," she said, with a chuckle. "Looks like a good life to me. This is what I was expecting the yachting life would be like. How long do you think you'll do this? Got any plans for after you get tired of sailing?"

"No. I just take it as it comes. How about you? Planning your next adventure already?"

"No, I just got here. I can't count the time on *Sisyphus*. I could do a lot more of this kind of sailing. And Puerto Rico's the only island I've seen."

"Puerto Rico's not typical," I said. "It's beautiful, but it's big, and it's part of the U.S. Wait until you see some of the Windwards and Leewards."

"How about the Virgins?"

"They're nice, but they're crowded and touristy. Not to mention expensive."

"Are there a lot of people like you down here, Finn?"

I frowned. "What are you asking?"

"People I could hitch rides with, just... you know, regular people?"

"I don't know. There are all kinds of people cruising the islands. Guess you'll have to see how it goes. Tired of my company already?"

"Oh, no! Not at all. I just don't want to wear out my welcome with you. And I was hoping to be able to make a little money along the way, but that's secondary."

"Well, you're welcome aboard *Island Girl* for as long as you can stand me. But if you want to move on, I understand. You're young, yet. Lots of adventures ahead of you."

She leaned in and gave me another kiss on the cheek.

"You're sweet, Finn. And I like you a lot; you don't seem so old to me. Thanks again for helping me out."

She picked up the dishes and turned to the companionway. I stood and tapped her on the shoulder. She jumped, surprised, and turned around. I took the dishes from her.

"I'll clean up the galley and sack out for a while, if you're okay taking the helm."

She grinned and nodded. "You got it, skipper."

8

IT ONLY TOOK ME A FEW MINUTES TO SQUARE AWAY THE GALLEY. I poked my head up through the companionway to see if Mary Beth needed anything before I went to sleep.

She was leaning back against the leeward side of the cockpit, her foot on the tiller. Head back, the breeze ruffling her curls, she watched a frigate bird gliding along in the slipstream from our sails. She was the picture of contentment.

I watched her for several seconds, reluctant to disturb her. She sensed my presence and looked over at me, smiling.

"You okay for a while?" I asked. "Need anything before I crash?"

"No, thanks. I'm fine, having a glorious sail. Get some rest."

"Yell if you need me, then."

I crawled into the sea berth and rolled to put my back against the lee cloth. With my knees drawn up against the back cushions, I steadied myself against *Island Girl's* rolling.

My head cradled in a pillow, I draped my left forearm over my eyes to block the light. I didn't drop off to sleep, though. I was still pondering how I'd come to have Mary Beth's company.

Her answers to my questions did nothing more than whet

my curiosity. I didn't learn much about her, at least not much of consequence.

The story of her travels since college was vague. My guess was that her folks left her with some money when they died, but if so, why did she want to pick up work as paid crew? Did she run through her inheritance?

And how long should I ignore her obvious flirtation? Did she really find me attractive, or was she playing me? And if she was playing me, why?

I told her I was happy to have her along for as long as she wanted. But she was curious about whether she could hitch rides on other boats. That could be an effort to avoid appearing too eager to impose on my hospitality. Or her entire story could be fabricated.

Nothing she told me explained the three men who jumped us in Puerto Real. The more I thought about them, the less likely it seemed that I was their target. I was there for a week before Mary Beth showed up. They could have moved on me any time; they wouldn't have waited until I had company.

I wondered again if she could have been part of a setup. If she were in league with those three, she didn't hold back when she pretended to help fight them off.

One suffered a dislocated knee, and the other's jaw was broken. That was more evidence that they were after her rather than me.

She said she couldn't connect them to *Sisyphus*. As she mentioned, if they were friends of the jerks on the superyacht, they wouldn't have followed her for days before making their move. Unless...

They were motivated by something other than revenge for what she did to the mate. That might be, but what other motive could they have?

Was there more to the *Sisyphus* tale than she told me? That could well be. A yacht like that was a multimillion-dollar investment. It would most likely have been run in a businesslike manner. Most people hired as deckhands on megayachts had some professional credentials, or at least relevant experience. As far as I knew, Mary Beth had neither.

She might have been hired based on some personal relationship with the captain or the owner, but that didn't fit the situation she described. The captain could have promised employment to lure her aboard for nefarious reasons. But Mary Beth didn't seem naïve enough to fall for that kind of thing. Besides, that wouldn't explain the three men who attacked us. For all I knew, there was no such vessel as *Sisyphus*. She could have made that up. But to what end?

I should have taken a closer look at her passport, but doing that now would be awkward. If she told the truth about arriving in Puerto Rico from the States, her passport wouldn't have any stamps for that trip anyway.

Only if she arrived from outside the U.S. would the passport tell me anything. It might corroborate her story of globetrotting for a year, but I didn't care about that.

As I was about to drop off, I realized that Mary Beth had the earmarks of an undercover operative. Her vague past, her enigmatic answers to some of my questions, and her hand-to-hand combat skills fit the pattern. That woke me up.

If she were a government agent, our encounter was surely pre-planned. That would mean whoever she worked for had access to my client contact person, because no one else in the government knew where to find me. But in that case, my contact would have told me. Unless...

Could they have decided I knew too much? Was Mary Beth here to make my retirement permanent? I shook my head.

She passed up a perfect opportunity when I fell asleep in the cockpit while she was steering earlier. Whatever she might be, she wasn't here to do me any harm.

Could she be part of a parallel operation? One that my

immediate contact didn't know about? Given the secrecy surrounding my department, that was a remote possibility.

I've dealt with the same client contact for nearly 20 years. While we've never met face-to-face, her track record with me is rock-solid. She wouldn't suddenly betray our mutual trust. If she knew about an operation that could affect my mission, she would have told me.

Mary Beth wasn't part of any government operation. After 20 years, I could just tell. So, I didn't need to call in and have her checked out. I still wondered about her, though. She knew more about what those guys in Puerto Real were up to than she told me. But there would be time to resolve that later, if we were to have a later.

My encounter with Mary Beth must be coincidental. But I would still keep probing her until I made sense of her story. I remembered the sage advice from a long-ago mentor; "If your mother says she loves you, check it out."

I resolved not to pass up any more opportunities to get to know her better. After all, she was sending signals that she would welcome my attention, and we were a couple of days from Bequia. And I really did find her attractive on more than one level.

9

I WAS ON WATCH FOR SUNRISE ON THE FIFTH MORNING OF OUR voyage. When I was far out at sea, I would argue with myself about whether sunsets or sunrises were more beautiful. If I were deprived of anything besides that split-second view when the horizon cuts across the sun, I might be hard pressed to tell the difference. There was no way to test that, though. There were always other sensory clues. The wind and the waves coupled with my sea sense always gave away whether the sun was coming or going.

That fifth sunrise was spectacular. In the tropics, the transition from night to day came quickly. Dawn was brief, just long enough to warn me that something was changing. Then a glorious, fiery ball would pop up on the horizon. As the sun climbed, it appeared to rest atop a column of gold that grew from the sea at my feet. Then the column vanished, and the new day was mine.

This particular sunrise interrupted my musing about what was to become of my relationship with Mary, which sprung up as quickly as the tropical sunrise. I smiled as I recollected her warning back in Puerto Real about that *thing* that happens between men and women. She turned out to be quite a woman.

The tattoos were out of character. She didn't seem like the type, but maybe I was just an old fuddy-duddy. The one on her hip wasn't so strange, once I got a better look at it.

It was a detailed sketch of Medusa. In the absence of the other one, it might not have been remarkable, but there was still the snake theme. The tattoo of the cobra, though... Well, I still couldn't figure out why a sweet girl like her had such a fearsome —

"Good morning, Finn," she said, handing me a steaming cup of coffee.

"Thanks." I must have been drowsing; I didn't hear her moving around below. "Glad you didn't miss the sunrise."

"Me, too," she said. "What put that smile on your face?"

"Coffee and a new day," I said.

"Bullshit. I've been watching you while the coffee perked. You've been grinning like a fool ever since there was enough light for me to see."

"Just happy, I reckon." I took a sip of the coffee as she settled in beside me on the windward cockpit seat.

"Me, too," she said. "It's been a great ride. What time do you think we'll make landfall?"

I shrugged. "Three or four hours, last time I looked. You didn't plot our position while the coffee was brewing?"

"I didn't want to break the spell. I was worried that if I turned on the light over the chart table, you'd notice. Then I wouldn't have been able to watch you." She gave me a little peck on the cheek. "What's on the agenda when we get to Bequia?"

"Well, after we clear in, I was thinking we might walk around a little. You been there before?"

"No. Just read about it. It sounds pretty different."

"Yep. It's a magical place. There's nowhere else like it. It's way different from St. Vincent."

"But it's only, what, twelve miles away?"

"About that. And there's a lot of traffic back and forth. I mean, it's the same country. People commute to work on the St. Vincent ferry, some of them. But it's like a different world, St. Vincent is. Ask any of the people in Bequia."

"I will. Can I buy you lunch ashore?"

"Sure. That'll be great. There's a place I know that serves good local food, and it's inexpensive. Run by an interesting woman, too. You'll enjoy her."

She smiled and took a sip of coffee. We passed several minutes in comfortable silence, and my thoughts drifted back to how this was going to play out.

So far, I kept my plans from her, but I needed to be on that ferry to St. Vincent tomorrow morning. That would put me there 24 hours earlier than I planned, which suited me well. I could handle my business and get out before anybody was the wiser.

"We need to talk, Finn." Her brow was furrowed as she looked me in the eye.

"Okay. What's on your mind?" Now I was a little worried.

"About us. You and me."

"Okay." I braced myself.

"Relax," she said, smiling. She shifted her gaze to the horizon. "I really like you. I mean a lot. But I'm not looking for anything long-term, okay?"

I nodded. "Okay. I figured that."

"I'm glad things worked out the way they have between us, but I don't want to impose on you. I need a little time alone while we're in Bequia. Is that all right?"

"Yeah," I said. "Sure. I understand."

She looked at me again, holding my eye for several seconds.

"Maybe you do. I hope so. Now, you were planning to come here before you met me, right?"

"Well, more or less. Somewhere in the neighborhood, anyhow."

"So, I'm guessing you have stuff to do here," she said. I frowned, and she went on.

"I'm not prying. What I want to say is that you should do what you need to do. I'll take care of myself. You don't need to worry about me."

Trying to figure out whether relief or regret was my dominant feeling, I put on my best poker face. "Is this goodbye, then?"

"It could be, if that's what you need. I don't want you to feel responsible for me. But if I won't be in your way, I wouldn't mind hanging out on *Island Girl* for a while."

"That's no problem. There are things I have to do; I'll be away for a day or two, after tomorrow morning. Make yourself at home. I'm happy to have you look after the boat, actually."

"Thanks, Finn. I'll take care of her as long as I can, but I have to tell you, I'll be looking for a crew position. It's not a reflection on you; it's just what I need to do."

I nodded. "We'd better talk to the customs and immigration people, then. We may need to do a little paper work, in case you find something before I get back."

"I'm not sure I understand," she said.

"We'll need to get you off the paperwork for *Island Girl* before you can leave on another boat. It won't be a big deal if I'm here. But if you find a slot before I get back, it could be a headache unless we prepare in advance."

"I see. Aside from my plans, how long are you planning to stay here?"

"Once I take care of my business, I'll be out of here. Unless you've found something, you're welcome to come along. I hope you will; I like you, Mary Beth."

"Yeah. I know. I like you, too. Let's just see how this turns out, okay?"

I nodded.

"I probably won't find anything in Bequia — not enough crewed charter yachts there. I'll have better luck somewhere like St. Lucia. I've read that there's more big-boat traffic around Rodney Bay. Or maybe Martinique. I'd be tickled to tag along with you to wherever you go next, if that's all right."

"Suits me fine," I said, smiling. "Should we do that paperwork with customs, just in case?"

She shrugged. "If it's not too complicated. It never hurts to hedge your bets."

"Amen to that," I said. "You want to take the helm? I'll go rustle up breakfast for us."

She gave me a kiss on the cheek and took the tiller from me.

10

Mary Beth was standing on the Bequia town dock, waving goodbye as the ferry to Kingstown pulled away. I stood at the rail on the upper deck, watching her until I couldn't pick her out of the crowd any longer. As much as I didn't want to, I admitted to myself that I would miss her while we were apart.

I haven't allowed myself the luxury of becoming attached to a woman in 20 years. I once had a wife and a daughter. Back then, I bought a house in the suburbs, trying to lock down my share of the American dream. But that didn't end well.

We married right after college, before I went on active duty. When my daughter was born, I was crawling on my belly in the jungle in one of those places the government still won't talk about. By the time I was extracted and returned to what passed for a safe place, my daughter was two months old.

I got the notice of her birth and arranged a phone call home, but the number was disconnected. That situation got worse before it got better. "Got better" was relative, and it took a long time -- years. Years when I wondered about my daughter. I didn't wonder about her mother; I knew how she felt about me. The lawyers made that clear right from the start.

I shook off the memories and turned from the rail, working my way to a seat on the open upper deck. It was early enough so that the sun wasn't too hot for me to enjoy sitting outside. Thinking about Mary Beth, I watched the shoreline of St. Vincent change from a gray smudge on the horizon to gray-green details as the ferry drew closer.

Mary Beth and I spent yesterday walking around Bequia. We acted like tourists and were mistaken for honeymooners by the shopkeepers. I felt easy with that. She made me feel good about life. I didn't want to think about her finding a crew berth and parting ways with me.

But I didn't have much to offer a woman. Woman — she was only a few years older than my daughter. I needed to get a grip, keep my perspective. What could she see in an old man like me? Even aside from the parts of my life I couldn't share with anybody, I was old enough to be her father. She was a breath of fresh air awakening hopes I suppressed for years.

But to her, I was sure I was just part of her current environment, one more piece of whatever puzzle she was working on. Not that I doubt the sincerity of the affection she expressed toward me, but I knew too much more about life to rely on her feelings *du jour*.

Glancing at my watch, I saw we would be landing in Kingstown in a half hour. I buried my thoughts about Mary Beth. She was a distraction I couldn't afford for the next couple of days. I had work to do, and wondering whether Mary Beth and I had a future could get me killed.

My target in Kingstown was a man who called himself Willi Dimitrovsky. He may have been Bulgarian, but no one was sure. He appeared out of nowhere, feeding large amounts of money into some whacked-out groups of extremists in the States.

His allegiance wasn't known for sure, but he was suspected of working for Russia. Whoever he represented, he was distributing large amounts of money to organizations at both ends of the political spectrum. His agenda appeared to be fomenting anarchy in the U.S.

St. Vincent was a hub for the drug trade in the Caribbean. That meant there were well-developed channels for funneling untraceable funds into and out of the States. That was probably why Dimitrovsky set up shop in Kingstown. He may have been smuggling drugs to fund his political activity, but it was the political meddling that put the target on his back.

He was running a grungy little seaman's bar called the Jolly Mon Tavern in one of the less savory parts of Kingstown. The word was that you could satisfy almost any appetite at the Jolly Mon. He lived in a villa in an upscale area, and he had the fix in with the authorities. His office was in the back room of the bar, and he had two eastern European thugs who served as his muscle.

It was going to appear that Willi was killed by a rival drug kingpin. That was my role in the play.

My first challenge was to figure out how to get an audience with Willi. I needed to get inside his back room. That's why I wanted to get to Kingstown a day early.

My last intelligence on Willi said he was leaving St. Vincent in three days, heading for Europe. That was why I picked tomorrow for the execution. We didn't want him in Europe. St. Vincent was a much better place for him to die, for several reasons.

The ferry was approaching the dock in Kingstown. I headed for the lounge where several people were finishing breakfast. Buying a cup of coffee, I sat down next to the exit door and waited for everyone to queue up to go ashore. I planned to lose myself in the crowd, just in case.

11

AFTER I DISEMBARKED FROM THE FERRY, I CHANGED CLOTHES IN the men's room in Kingstown's public market. I put on a faded, stained T-shirt and a pair of greasy blue jeans that were worn through at the knees. In place of my scuffed boat shoes, I slipped on a pair of worn running shoes that were once light gray. I stuffed my good clothes into my oil-stained duffle bag.

From the sink in front of the shattered mirror, I scraped up a little grime and rubbed it into the unkempt stubble on my nut-brown face. Pulling on a ratty straw hat, its brim in tatters, I slung the bag over my shoulder and stepped back out into the market. The disgusted looks I got from the women tending their stalls told me my disguise was a success.

Before I left the immediate area of the market, I found a trash tip that reeked of rotting fish and smeared a little slime on my T-shirt. On my way from the market to the Jolly Mon Tavern, I stopped in a couple of scruffy watering holes, spilling most of my cheap rum drinks on my clothes.

I was in a filthy room in a guest house across the street from the Jolly Mon Tavern. By the time I got there, no one would have guessed that I was anything but a drunken deck hand

from a commercial fishing vessel. When I checked in, the desk
clerk wrinkled his nose and asked for my passport.

"We put in the safe," he said, "Jus' to be sure."

I gave my head a confused shake and handed him $50 E.C.
in soiled, small-denomination notes.

The clerk folded the money into his pocket instead of
putting my passport in the safe. He charged me another $50
E.C. for a room for the night, rattling off a litany of forbidden
activities. I asked him for my room key.

He laughed. "No locks, mon. Only honest people stay here.
No one gon' mess wit' you, prob'ly. Up those stairs, firs' door on
the lef'."

There was a clear view of the Jolly Mon Tavern through the
room's one window. Most of the glass was broken out; what was
left was flyspecked. Typically, there was no screen, and the flies
liked the way I smelled. The room was marginally bearable; I
put up with worse. I was stretched out on the stained sheets,
propped up enough so I could watch the entrance to the
Jolly Mon.

It was mid-morning, and there was no activity at the tavern.
I was surprised; it looked like the kind of place where people
who looked like me would go to start their day. As I stumbled
past the tavern's door on my way here, I noticed it was
padlocked.

If I didn't see a sign of life by early afternoon, I would ask
around and see if it was still in business. If not, then I would
buy a prepaid phone and check in with my client. I left my
phone on *Island Girl*. People who look like me didn't carry
iPhones. That would have blown my cover for sure.

A dented SUV pulled to a stop at the curb in front of the
Jolly Mon. The windows were heavily tinted, but the driver, a
black man with a shaved head, had his window rolled halfway
down. A burly white man got out of the front passenger door.
He was looking up and down the sidewalk, one hand on what

must have been a pistol in his waistband under his untucked sport shirt.

He looked back into the SUV and nodded before closing the door. Walking to the entrance of the tavern, he unlocked the padlock and opened the door. He disappeared inside for almost a minute. Then he came back outside, standing in the doorway. He gave an offhand wave, and the rear passenger door of the SUV opened.

Another burly white man stepped out, looking both ways, again with a hand on a concealed pistol. He said something I couldn't hear, and Willi Dimitrovsky got out and hustled to the tavern entrance. He was a careful man, or maybe he heard rumors about somebody gunning for him. I hoped it was the former, but it didn't change what I had to do.

The SUV pulled away and turned at the next corner, probably headed for a parking place behind the Jolly Mon. I was a little surprised that Willi didn't use the back entrance if he was worried about security. On my way to the hotel earlier, I poked my head into the alley that ran behind the tavern. Maybe Willi didn't like it because the alley was a dead end; there was only one way in and out.

About two minutes passed, and then the black man with the shaved head came up the sidewalk, accompanied by a heavy-set, middle-aged black man and a young woman. From her scanty attire, I guessed she was the barmaid. I was a little surprised by that. People in the islands are pretty conservative when it comes to dress. She would look at home in Vegas, but she was out of place in Kingstown, even at the sleaziest joint in town. The heavy-set man was carrying a stack of three rectangular foam plastic containers — take-out breakfast or lunch, I guessed.

My original plan was to wait until the place was busy enough for me to blend in with the clientele while I had a drink and checked things out. Seeing that Willi was there, and the place had no customers, I decided to move the schedule up a little. Somebody had to be their first customer of the day, and I wouldn't have to worry about bystanders if I struck while the place was empty.

I took the razor-sharp 12-inch filet knife out of my duffle bag and strapped its sheath to the inside of my left calf. Feeling around in the bag, I found the coiled, three-foot length of two-hundred-pound-test stainless steel wire leader. It had a half-ounce lead sinker on each end. That was an odd way to rig a leader for fishing, but it made a perfect garrote, and it wouldn't arouse suspicion if someone saw it. Neither would the knife, except that it was hidden under my pants, strapped to my lower leg. That wasn't where a fisherman would have carried his knife, but I wanted to conceal it.

I slung the duffle bag over my shoulder and went downstairs. The desk clerk wasn't around. I let myself out the front door and paused, looking around like a drunk hunting the closest liquor. Grinning, I locked my eyes on the door of the Jolly Mon Tavern and stepped off the curb. I staggered a little crossing the street, in case anyone was watching.

The interior of the bar was about what I expected. The two white men were sitting in a booth, eating scrambled eggs from the take-out containers. The middle-aged black man was behind the bar. The three of them checked me out, and the two white men went back to their food. I figured Willi was in his office, but the barmaid wasn't in sight. I wasn't sure what to do about her yet, anyway. The black man with the shaved head was missing, too.

The bartender studied me as I approached him, his eyes sending the signal that I didn't belong there. "Not open yet," he said, leaning on the bar, both of his beefy arms straight, hands folded into fists.

"How 'bout a couple beers to go," I asked, giving him a loopy grin.

He shook his head, staring at me. I kept grinning, swaying a little. I took out my rumpled wad of E.C. notes and counted out $20, dropping it on the bar. I raised my eyebrows, and he shrugged. I put another $20 on the bar. He swept up the bills and turned, dropping the money into a cigar box behind the bar.

Reaching down, he picked up two bottles of Carib and set them on the bar in front of me. Putting my duffle bag on the bar, I unzipped it. I picked up one beer and put it in the bag while he went back to leaning on the bar, his weight on his arms again. I reached over and picked up the second beer by the neck, flipping my hand at the last minute.

He frowned, trying to make sense of my odd grip. I uncoiled my tensed muscles, swinging the bottle in a backhand that struck him on the side of his head. His eyes rolled back, and he slipped out of sight, collapsing behind the bar in slow motion.

The beer still in my grip, I whirled and leapt across the narrow space between me and the two men in the booth. I smashed the beer into the back of one white man's head with enough force to break the bottle. The other one put his hand on his pistol. He was struggling to free it from his waistband when I cut his throat with the broken bottle. Then I smashed my left fist into his chin. He would bleed to death while he was unconscious.

The man I hit from behind fell face-first into his scrambled eggs. I grabbed his hair in my left fist and pulled his head back, cutting his throat with the bottle too. I helped myself to their pistols, sticking one in my waist at the small of my back, holding the other. Nine-millimeter Glocks. No safety to get in my way.

I stepped around behind the bar and cut the bartender's throat with my filet knife. I wasn't sure what his role was, but I couldn't afford to leave a witness. I took a one-liter plastic bottle of club soda from the refrigerator and twisted off the cap, pouring the contents down the sink. Then I went looking for Willi.

I walked through the open door at the end of the bar, looking for the back room. It was at the end of a short hall. Willi looked up just as I entered his office. The man with the shaved head was sitting in front of the desk facing Willi, his back to me. When he saw the surprised look on Willi's face, he turned and saw me. He was reaching for his pistol as he tried to stand. I held the neck of the empty soda bottle over the muzzle of the Glock and pulled the trigger four times — two for Willi, two for his friend. The soda bottle wasn't as good as a real suppressor, but it did an okay job of silencing the pistol, considering we were inside. It was doubtful that anyone outside heard the shots. There was still no sign of the barmaid. That was just as well. It was her lucky day.

Willi's friend was missing most of the back of his head, but Willi took his two shots to the heart. I reached down and checked Willi's neck for a pulse, just to be sure about him. He wouldn't be stirring up any more trouble with the extremists in the States. Back out at the bar, I found a damp rag to wipe down the two pistols. I wrapped each one in its owner's hand and left the two dead thugs at the table. Then I wiped my prints off the soda bottle and the broken beer bottle, leaving both on the table.

My mission accomplished a day ahead of my plan, I strolled back to the city market. I resumed my identity as a cruising yachtsman in the men's room there and caught the next ferry back to Bequia. I figured I would surprise Mary Beth and take her out for a nice meal at the French restaurant.

12

As the ferry pulled into Bequia's Admiralty Bay, I spotted *Island Girl* at anchor over near Princess Margaret Beach. We were too far away for me to make out much detail, but the dinghy was trailing off her stern. I thought Mary Beth must be aboard.

If I had a phone, I could have called her to pick me up at the town dock. No, I guess I couldn't; I didn't have her cellphone number. Thinking about it, I realized I didn't even know if she had a phone. Surely, she must; didn't everybody have one?

I made my way down to the main deck as the ferry slowed and swung around, the engines revving in reverse. The captain was backing into the town dock. As soon as the ramp went down, I worked my way through the crowd on the dock and walked to where the water taxis were waiting.

I boarded a water taxi, and in a few minutes we were alongside *Island Girl*. I paid the operator and scrambled over *Island Girl's* lifelines. As the water taxi pulled away, I called out to Mary Beth, surprised that she didn't come on deck to see what the disturbance was.

There was no answer. I dropped my duffle bag and went

down the companionway ladder. She wasn't aboard, and the main cabin was in disarray. There was a plate on the cabin sole, the remains of a half-eaten sandwich near it. A soft-drink bottle was on its side, rolling across the saloon table with the motion of the boat. There was a sticky splotch of stale, drying soda pop on the tabletop.

Frowning, I checked the forward cabin. She wasn't there. I opened the locker where she kept her backpack. It was still there, so she didn't find a crew berth during the few hours I was gone.

Worried, I did a more careful examination of the main cabin. Nothing appeared to be missing. Our passports were still in the drawer under the chart table with the ship's papers, in their clear vinyl envelope.

As I stepped onto the companionway ladder, leaning out into the cockpit to retrieve my bag, I noticed the reddish-brown smear on the ladder's top right handgrip. I moistened my fingertip with saliva and ran it across the stain, watching as it smeared. It was dried blood, but was it hers or someone else's?

I reached out and grabbed my duffle bag, taking it to the forward cabin and tossing it on the V-berth. Opening the second drawer under the nav station, I found my iPhone. That's where it stayed most of the time. I turned it on and watched as it powered up. I was trying to decide what I should do next.

The phone had a good signal, but there were no texts or voicemails. I dropped it in my pocket. The keyring with its orange foam float was hanging by the companionway opening. I took it off its hook and climbed into the cockpit. I would take the dinghy into town. As I was unlocking the dinghy, it occurred to me to take our passports and papers; I went below to get them.

Back in the dinghy, I cranked the outboard. At the noise, a man poked his head up through the companionway of the boat anchored about 75 feet off our starboard side. Nosy neighbor, I thought, giving him a smile and a wave. He waved back, and I steered the dinghy over to his boat and killed the engine.

"Good afternoon," I said, as I drifted alongside.

"Afternoon," he said, climbing into his boat's cockpit.

"I'm Finn, from *Island Girl*. You been here long?"

"I'm Dave," he said. "Good to meet you, Finn. We got here a couple of days ago. Saw you guys come in yesterday, but you left before we could welcome you to the neighborhood."

"Yeah; first time here for my lady. We did a little sightseeing."

"Uh-huh," Dave said. "We saw you leave this morning while we were gettin' breakfast together. Thought we'd stop over and say hello to your wife later. We saw her come back after she took you ashore."

"She's not here," I said. "I wondered if you saw her leave."

"No. She came back about the time the first ferry left the harbor. The wife and I were gonna swing by and visit after we ate, but by then, there was a speedboat with two guys and a woman alongside your boat. We went on into town to buy groceries. When we got back, the speedboat was gone and your dinghy was there, so we rapped on the hull, but she didn't answer. Figured the folks in the speedboat must be friends of yours, and she caught a ride to town with them."

"What kind of speedboat? One of the water taxis?"

"No, it was one of those rentals, like from the marina over there in the corner of the harbor. Little fiberglass tri-hull — maybe 12 or 13 feet — with a 25-horse Mercury."

"I better go see if I can catch up with her, then," I said. "Good to meet you, Dave. Maybe we'll see you later."

"Sure, Finn. You folks stop by any time. We're most always aboard."

I started the outboard and headed for the marina, hoping they were still open. Maybe I could find out who the people were.

I was no more than a hundred yards from *Island Girl* when my phone rang. I pulled it from my pocket and throttled back the outboard while I checked the caller ID. I didn't recognize the number, but the first three digits were 784, the country code for St. Vincent and the Grenadines. I accepted the call and held the phone to my ear, killing the outboard so I could hear.

"Yeah?"

"Hey, Finn, it's me."

"Mary Beth? What's going on?"

"It's a long story. The main thing is there are two people looking for me. I need to get off the island."

"Okay. I'm ready to go; I finished my business. Can I pick you up?"

"Not a good idea," she said. "Too much chance they're watching you from somewhere. They were in a little rental speedboat."

"Our neighbor said there were three of them. Two men and a woman."

"He's right. There were. The woman's dead. This is her phone. The other two are in town; we're staying in touch by text. They're watching the waterfront for our dinghy. Don't go there."

"What do you mean, 'we're staying in touch by text?'"

"Yeah, we are. They think I'm her."

"Where are you?"

"Not far. I'm at the beach bar around the point from Princess Margaret beach. The one behind the big reef at the west end of the anchorage where you are."

"They can't see that from town. I can — "

"No. There's more, but I'll tell you later. Go back to the boat. I'll swim out; I shouldn't be more than a few minutes behind you. We need to get the hell out of here. Please?"

"Let's go," I said. "See you in a few minutes."

I put the phone in my pocket and fired up the outboard,

heading back to *Island Girl*. I thought about taking the outboard off the dinghy and stowing it for sea, but decided that might be risky if Mary Beth was right. They could be watching *Island Girl* from a number of places.

We could tow the dinghy until we were out of sight of town and then bring it aboard. There was still the question of how Mary Beth could get aboard with no one noticing, though. I shrugged that off for now. We would think of something.

I tied the dinghy to the stern rail and climbed aboard *Island Girl*. Uncovering the sails, I got them ready for a quick departure.

I just finished folding the mainsail cover and stashing it in the port cockpit locker when I heard Mary Beth call my name in a quiet tone.

"Yeah," I said, standing up.

"Don't look around," she said. "Pull the dinghy along the starboard side."

"Okay," I said, turning to untie the dinghy painter. She gave me a big smile. Her head was tucked under the bow of the inflatable.

"How are we going to get you aboard?"

"If you put the dinghy on the starboard side, *Island Girl* will block the view from town. I'll just roll into the dinghy and lie flat, and you can tow it along shore until we're far enough out. Then let *Island Girl* drift while we bring it aboard, okay?"

"Okay." I untied the painter and pulled the dinghy around as she suggested, making it fast to the side of *Island Girl* with bow and stern lines.

She rolled into the inflatable. "Thanks, Finn."

"Glad to see you," I said. "I'll just motor down to the cove off Moonhole — only be a few minutes."

"Whatever you think," she said.

13

Ten minutes later, we stowed the dinghy and put up the mainsail. There wasn't much breeze yet, so we resumed motor sailing along the south shore of Admiralty Bay.

"Okay," I said. "Now tell me what happened."

"Not long after I got back from taking you to the ferry, I was hungry, so I made an early lunch. There were two men who came aboard, and a woman who waited in their boat. I broke the first one's nose and gave the other a good shot to his family jewels. Before they recovered, I took off.

"When I went topside, the woman was there, holding a gun on me. I dove over the side and swam as far as I could underwater. By the time they regrouped, I was hiding in the undergrowth along the beach.

"They rode around the anchorage for a while, looking for me, then they dropped the woman on the beach and headed for town. She was standing there looking at *Island Girl* when I broke her neck and took her phone. They kept texting updates to one another every ten or fifteen minutes. That's about it."

"Did you recognize them?"

"No. They weren't from *Sisyphus,* if that's what you were thinking."

"Too bad you didn't get to question the woman."

"It would have been too risky. As it was, I was lucky to get the drop on her before people started coming to the beach club."

"Did you bring her phone?"

"Yes, but it's a prepaid throwaway." Mary Beth pulled a plastic bag with the phone in it from her pocket. "No numbers in the directory except the other two."

"Names?"

"Derek Jacobs and Len Woods. The woman was Kathy, but I don't have a last name for her."

"You said she had a pistol."

She reached behind her back and pulled a Glock 19 from her waistband. She popped the magazine and racked the slide, catching the extra round that ejected from the chamber. "Want it?" she asked.

"Not much," I said, noticing how familiar she was with the pistol. "You might as well hang on to it until we're sure we're clear of the two men, but we should ditch it in deep water. More trouble than it's worth, down here."

She nodded. "Thanks for saving me again, Finn. I owe you twice, now."

"Glad to help," I said. "You sure you don't want to tell me what's going on?"

She frowned for a few seconds. "I'm still trying to work it out. I'd rather wait until I've got a better idea myself. Is that a problem for you?"

I shook my head. "I'm a good listener, when you get ready."

She nodded. "I know you are. I appreciate your patience with me. I hope I haven't screwed up your business here."

I shook my head. "Nope. Got done way ahead of time. That's why I'm back early."

"My good fortune. I wasn't looking forward to sleeping on the beach for a night or two."

"Guess it was meant to be," I said.

"You believe in luck?"

I shrugged. "I believe stuff happens that's beyond your control, stuff you can't anticipate. It can be good or bad, depending."

"Depending on what?"

"Mostly on how you react to it, I reckon."

"Did you hear about the murders?" she asked.

I gave her a blank look and shook my head, poker face in place. "What murders?"

"In Kingstown, this morning. I heard about them on the local TV news; it was playing at the beach bar."

"You were in the bar?" I asked.

"I was hiding in the scrub outside. Five men killed in a waterfront bar that caters to merchant seamen. Three in the bar with their throats cut, two in the office shot with a pistol that belonged to one of the men out front."

"There are some rough places in Kingstown," I said.

She looked into my eyes for several beats. She reached out and took my right hand, holding it in her lap. "I gathered that. I was worried about you." She squeezed my hand.

"Thanks, but I'm okay. They say anything else about the murders?"

"That's all they talked about. One of the men, a guy named Willi Dimitrovsky, was suspected of drug smuggling and money laundering. The U.S. has been trying to extradite him. The others were his bodyguards. Except the bartender. He just ran the bar for him."

"Who found them?"

"The barmaid. She was in the ladies' room when it happened. She heard the scuffle, but she was scared, so she stayed put until it got quiet."

"Smart lady."

"Yeah. She said they were just getting ready to open for the day."

"Any clues to who did it?"

"They're looking for a drunk who was seen in the area. He'd booked a room in a hotel across the street a little while before it happened. The desk clerk said he smelled like he worked on a fishing boat."

Neither of us said anything for a couple of minutes. I broke the silence. "About time to raise the jib and kill the diesel."

She jerked, startled, and gripped my hand.

"What's wrong?" I asked.

"It just hit me. We didn't clear out with customs and immigration," she said. "What can we do about that?"

"There are other places before we leave the waters of Saint Vincent and the Grenadines. We can clear out at Union Island and then go to Grenada."

She sighed. "That okay with you?"

"Sure," I said. "Let's get some sail up. We'll anchor for the night somewhere down near Union Island and clear out in the morning." I tried to retrieve my hand, but she held on, looking at it and frowning.

"That's dried blood around your fingernails," she said, turning my hand over and looking at my wrist and the inside of my forearm. "Did you cut yourself?"

"No."

"What happened?"

I shook my head. "Let's raise that jib."

"Finn? Did you have trouble of some kind?"

"I'm okay, Mary Beth. Let it go. No more questions, okay?"

"Aye, skipper." She dropped my hand and stood. "Let's get that jib up."

14

Once we were clear of the southwest tip of Bequia, we took up a southerly course and trimmed the sails. We settled in on a nice beam reach, making about five and a half knots. There was a moderate chop — just enough to keep the spray flying and break the monotony.

After a few minutes, Mary Beth asked, "You hungry?"

"I could eat," I said. "You cooking? Or am I?"

"I'll cook. I'm starving. Those bastards interrupted my lunch."

"Yeah, I noticed. I didn't take the time to clean up before I took off to look for you."

"That's okay. I'll get beans and rice cooking and straighten up below. Want a beer or anything before I get started?"

"No, thanks. I'm okay for now."

She went below and rustled around in the galley for a few minutes. I saw her lock the pots in place on the stove-top. She released the latch, allowing the stove to swing in its gimbals. Then she moved forward, disappearing from my view for a minute or two.

She poked her head through the companionway and smiled

at me as she tossed her stale sandwich over the side. Ducking below again, she washed the dish that I saw on the cabin sole, putting it away. Then she stuck her head up again.

"You okay for a little while?" she asked.

"Sure. Why?"

"I want to rinse off the salt and put on dry clothes while our dinner cooks. Maybe do a little laundry, if we can spare the water."

"Go for it," I said. "We can fill the tanks in Grenada easily enough."

I sailed along, enjoying the ride. The water pump cycled a few times as she showered and washed out her clothes.

While I had a little time to myself, I retrieved my satellite phone and sent a quick, coded text to my client. News of my success would have reached them already, but they needed to know I was in the clear. I debated adding a question or two about Mary Beth and then thought better of it. I pressed send and waited while the text went. Then I powered off the phone and put it away.

I was leaning back and steering with my foot when Mary Beth popped up on deck in her bikini, arms loaded with wet clothes. She fished around in the cockpit locker for the hank of small stuff that served as a clothesline.

Standing on the cockpit seat next to me, she leaned her hip into my shoulder to steady herself and reached up as high as she could stretch. She tied the clothesline to the backstay. Stepping out onto the side deck, she unrolled the line until she reached the weather shrouds. She looped the line around the shrouds a few times and carried it on up to the headstay. She tied the other end there.

"You must have had a lot of dirty clothes," I said, when she came back and picked up the first few items to hang on the line.

"Mostly yours," she said, giving me a hard look. "That stuff in your duffle bag reeked of dead fish and cheap liquor, like a drunk who worked on a fishing boat."

She finished hanging out the laundry and went below to check on our dinner, leaving me to ponder our situation. We both killed people in the last few hours, but I didn't plan to tell anybody about my activity. Mary Beth described sneaking up behind that woman and breaking her neck like it was no big deal.

But then the woman threatened Mary Beth, at least arguably. My victims didn't have an inkling that I was coming for them. Did that give Mary Beth some kind of moral advantage? Maybe. Then again, she'd drawn me into her mess, whatever it was. I didn't want her to poke her nose into my business.

I did what I went to Kingstown to do, and I left no evidence to connect me to the deaths. There would be no repercussions, unless Mary Beth voiced her suspicions to someone. Even then, I could argue that there were lots of drunks who smelled like dead fish.

I was less comfortable that the body Mary Beth left on the beach wouldn't be connected to us. A brawl in Puerto Rico was one thing; those men attacked us, and we didn't kill anybody. In the case of the woman Mary Beth killed, though, the optics were different.

To a witness who saw what happened on the beach, the woman was standing there minding her own business and watching the boats. Mary Beth attacked from behind, broke her neck, and hid the body. She also stole the woman's phone — and her pistol. But the pistol might be a liability to Mary Beth. Who could say she didn't have it when she attacked the woman?

"Penny?" Mary Beth said, putting two bowls of beans and rice on the bridge deck and climbing into the cockpit.

"What?" I shook my head, frowning.

"For your thoughts. You looked miles away." She handed me a bowl and a spoon and sat down, squeezing up against me.

"Yeah, I guess. Pondering our situation."

"What about it?"

"You did hide her body, right?"

"As best I could. Dragged it into the scrub and brushed out the tracks with palm fronds. Why?"

"Wondering if we're going to have any trouble, that's all."

"It was self-defense," she said.

"Maybe. But — "

"Hold on a second, Finn. They boarded our boat at gunpoint. Don't you dare give me any crap after what you did."

"Take it easy," I said. "I'm not going all moral on you. And you have no idea what I did or didn't do in Kingstown."

"Bullshit, Finn!"

I put a spoonful of beans and rice in my mouth and chewed, buying a few seconds. When she didn't say anything, I spoke.

"You have your suspicions about me. You think I killed those people. I get that. But you need to know that whatever I might have done, I'm clean from the standpoint of hard evidence. There's nothing to connect me to them. No witnesses, no fingerprints, nothing."

"So?"

"So, I understand you killed that woman because she was a threat to you."

"Kathy," she said. "Her name was Kathy."

"Did you know her?" I frowned. "I thought you said — "

"No, I didn't know her. But the least I can do is call her by her name. It makes it seem less..."

"You always call your victims by name?"

"Are you fishing?"

"Yes."

"Well, stop. That's rude. I'm not ready to share that much of my background with you yet."

"Yet?"

"Yes, yet. The time may come. And don't forget, she was the one with the gun."

"Let's back up a second, Mary Beth. I didn't mean to start an argument with you. I'm just worried about what an eyewitness to what happened on that beach might tell a cop." I stopped speaking and held her gaze for a moment.

"There wasn't anyone there but the two of us."

"Okay. But if somebody had seen it, from what you told me, you were the aggressor, as far as what happened on the beach."

She chewed her lower lip for a few seconds. Then she nodded. "Yeah, okay. I get it. You're worried we're going to get questioned?"

"It could happen," I said. "We don't know who saw what, as far as our departure. Let's say you're right, and nobody saw what happened on the beach. Somebody will find her body. Somebody may have spotted you hanging out in that area, even if they didn't connect you with her. Somebody — maybe just our nosy neighbor on the next boat — saw us leave. See what I mean?"

"Yeah. So, what should we do?"

"We need to get our act together, that's what. If the cops show up with questions, we shouldn't have any loose ends."

"You think they will?"

"They might. Bequia and Union Island are part of the same country. Neither one is very big. They could have put out the word to watch for *Island Girl*. We could get some questions in the morning when we clear out. Or not. Better to have a plan, though, in case they ask."

"You've done this kind of thing before," she said.

"No comment."

"Finn, I'm sorry I got you mixed up in my mess. You've been good to me. Maybe I should just bail out in Union Island."

I shook my head. "I don't think so. We're in this together."

"I'm fond of you, Finn. I know you're fond of me, but you don't need this, believe me. Cut your losses."

"Too late," I said. "And yes, I'm fond of you, but that's got nothing to do with it. We need each other to weather this little blow. Then we'll see about parting ways, if you want. Okay?"

She set her bowl down and snuggled up against me, her head on my shoulder. "Thanks, Finn. Parting ways isn't something I want. I guess it's time for me to tell you about what's going on with me."

15

"I don't even know where to start, Finn. My life's such a mess."

She was looking at me, waiting for a reaction. I kept my expression blank and gave her a little nod. After a few seconds, she spoke.

"My family — my parents, that is — were involved in organized crime. Mostly gambling, but once you're over the line, there aren't really any distinctions. Crooked is crooked, you know?"

I nodded.

"Later on, I found out they were into drugs, prostitution, you name it. My father wasn't, like, the Godfather, but he was definitely one of the lieutenants. I grew up in the middle of it all. Didn't really know the difference, I guess. There was lots of money, but everyone I knew had rich parents. My friends and I, we were spoiled brats. Except for my brother. He was different, but we'll get to that.

"When I was starting my senior year in college, I came home for a weekend visit and found my parents dead. Not just dead, but butchered. It was like something out of a horror movie. I freaked out and ran, but I didn't have a clue. Got in my car and took off. Nowhere to go, no money, except credit cards. I stopped for gas that night and discovered that the cards didn't work anymore. I was sleeping in my car somewhere in Alabama, begging and stealing gas money, when my brother found me."

"Tell me about your brother. He was wounded in Iraq, you said?"

She grimaced and shrugged. "He was in Iraq. He was a sniper, I guess. He was wounded, but nothing major. He was decorated for valor, and he was out by the time my parents were killed. But he wasn't staying with them. He was estranged from my parents. He's ten years older than I am. He left home and joined the Army when I was about eight. I hardly knew him until he came along and took me under his wing.

"He got out of the military and started teaching mixed martial arts; I was telling the truth about that. He was great at it. He took me in and made a home for me, got me back in school, whipped me into shape. I owe him a lot. Thanks to him, I was only a quarter late finishing school.

"He was a success at the MMA thing. He won all kinds of matches and ended up with his own gym. Then they came after us."

"They?"

"The people my parents were involved with."

"But why?" I asked. "What did they want with you two?"

"They thought he was keeping a bunch of files for my parents. I was back in college by then. They threatened me in order to get him to hand over whatever it was. But I didn't even know that about the threat. Two of them were following me around on campus. They sent him pictures of me, reminded him what happened to our parents. I was oblivious to it.

"The two guys following me were found dead on campus, overdosed on some kind of designer drug. I was still clueless, at that point. My brother never told me what was going on. Not until I was out of school. Things were quiet after that. For a while."

"Was he behind their deaths?" I asked.

"The two who were following me?"

"Right."

"Probably, but he wouldn't talk about it. He said it was wrong to ask someone a question like that. I mean, I know some of what he did in the military. He was a sniper, at one point. I remember hearing that from my parents. But I think he was more than just a regular sniper, at least later. Maybe an assassin."

I raised my eyebrows at that. "Did you make up the part about his disability?"

"Not exactly. Like I said, he was wounded in Iraq, but not seriously." I thought about that for several seconds as she ate a little of her dinner. When she finished chewing, I said, "Fast forward to a week ago, in Puerto Rico."

"Okay. What do you want to know?"

"How did you get there?"

"They kidnapped me off the street in Miami. I was held on *Sisyphus* for a couple of weeks. I got the drop on one of my guards in Fajardo and escaped. I was making the rounds of the places where cruising yachts hang out, trying to hitch a ride. I spotted you. I'm sorry, Finn. I shouldn't have gotten you caught up in this. You don't deserve it."

"Quit apologizing. It's a waste of time, at this point. And you have no idea what I deserve or don't deserve. Were the men in Puerto Real from *Sisyphus*?"

"I never saw them aboard her. They *could* have been, but I don't think so. Over the time I was there, I'm sure I got a look at everybody aboard."

"And you don't know who owns *Sisyphus*?"

"Not for sure, but I'd guess she belongs to O'Hanlon."

"O'Hanlon?"

"He's the head of the mob my family was connected to — like the Irish Mafia. Rory O'Hanlon. From Boston, originally."

"Never heard of him, but that doesn't mean much. When you jumped ship in Fajardo, what did you bring with you?"

"The clothes on my back. Why?"

"Where'd you get the backpack? And the passport?"

"Stole them. Not the passport. When I killed the guy watching me, he was carrying it. They were getting ready to send me somewhere. He was going to take me to the airport and escort me to wherever O'Hanlon wanted me. So I got lucky with that. I found a little cash on him, too. But the rest of my stuff, I picked up along the way. Why?"

"I thought maybe they'd planted a tracking device in your stuff. They found you in Bequia pretty damn quick. Any idea how?"

She frowned and shook her head. "No. I was wondering about that. I spotted those men in Puerto Rico early on. They were beating the bushes, showing people pictures, offering them money. The ones here came out of nowhere."

I nodded. "The passport — it's yours?"

She squinted and shook her head. "I don't — "

"I mean, did you have it before they kidnapped you in Miami? They didn't give it to you?"

"No. I mean, yes, I had it before. They took it away from me, but I'm sure it's the same one. It's got all the right stamps in it. Why?"

"Still trying to figure out how they tracked you to Bequia."

"Could they have followed us?" she asked.

"You mean from Puerto Rico?"

"Yes," she said.

"In theory, yes, I guess they could have. But then why wait

until we got here to make their move? They could have nailed us at sea with no witnesses."

"Good point. But where does that leave us?"

"In the dark, for now. How big is O'Hanlon's operation?"

"I don't know. Big, I think."

"Big enough to have people on his payroll in the islands?" I asked. "You said he was into drugs."

"I don't know, Finn. Maybe. What are you thinking?"

"I'm just trying out ideas, wondering if he's got enough stroke to have somebody on his payroll in customs and immigration. Maybe in each of the countries that are major transshipment points for drugs into the U.S. St. Vincent fits that description. That's happened before with big-time drug smugglers."

"If that's so, what about Grenada?" she asked.

"I don't know. It's possible, but less likely, to my mind. Grenada's not as much of a crossroads for drugs. Tell me about the three people who boarded *Island Girl*."

"What about them?"

"Black, white, Asian? Local? American? Any accents? Anything at all that you remember. I'm trying to figure out if they were recruited nearby or sent in from elsewhere, for starters."

"Well, they were black, and they spoke a *patois*. English with a little French mixed in. One of the men was light-skinned, with these eerie green eyes. Except for the scars on his face, he would have been stunning. He was slender, but muscular. He seemed to be in charge. He's the one whose nose I broke. The others weren't as distinctive looking. Does that help?"

"Maybe, but not right now. They could have been locals, or from any of the islands, based on what you've told me so far. Think about it and let me know if you remember anything else about them."

"Okay. You finished dinner? I'll go clean up."

I handed her my bowl as she stood up. "It's a nice evening," I said. "We can anchor in Chatham Bay on the west side of Union Island. Should get in by 10:30 or 11:00. We'll get a good night's sleep and sail around to Clifton on the east side to clear out in the morning. Sound okay?"

"Sure," she said leaning down to kiss my cheek. "Thanks again, Finn."

"My pleasure."

16

WHILE MARY BETH SQUARED AWAY THE GALLEY, I THOUGHT about my options. I was between missions; my time was my own. Mary Beth was in trouble, but it wasn't my trouble. Not yet, anyway. I could cut her loose in Grenada, or take her to St. Lucia. She would stand a better chance of finding a crew slot there, if that's even what she wanted to do. I wasn't sure she was serious about that. If she was, St. Martin would offer even more opportunities for her that way. But I wasn't feeling good about cutting her loose.

I was attached to her. Having a lady in my life was nice for a change. She liked me well enough, but I wasn't sure she was interested in any permanent relationship. I was out of practice at this kind of thing, and then there was the generation gap, too. People her age were more casual about relationships than old bastards like me.

That could be a plus, her openness. She would likely find it easier to talk about our prospects than I would. That wasn't my biggest worry, though. I knew deep down inside that I already made my mind up about her, and my gut said she felt the same way about me. If I was reading this wrong, she would let me know soon enough. I was all-in as far as keeping her around.

I knew that was just the beginning, though. She claimed not to know why O'Hanlon was after her, but I wondered about her brother. What did he know? And was she in touch with him?

Those questions could wait. We had more immediate problems. To stay safe long enough to solve the O'Hanlon puzzle, she needed a new identity. I could help with that, once we got past the personal side of things.

Given that O'Hanlon's people tracked her to Bequia, they would have me on their radar. Whoever they were, they were pros at this. They might have written off a single encounter with me like the one in Puerto Real. After they saw us together in Bequia, though, they would figure I was part of their problem. I knew how to deal with that, but before I did, I wanted to know exactly who I was up against. I needed to learn more about O'Hanlon and company.

The first thing was to reach an understanding with Mary Beth. As if on cue, she joined me in the cockpit.

"Nice evening," she said, as she settled in next to me on the windward cockpit seat. "At times like this, I feel like I could stay at sea forever."

"Yeah, I know the feeling. But every so often, you have to go ashore."

"I feel safe out here," she said.

"That's an illusion. Trouble can follow you anywhere. Whoever's after you knows by now that you're with me."

"I'm sorry, Finn."

"No need. Trouble and I have a long history. Some folks think I'm a carrier, even."

"A carrier?"

"Like Typhoid Mary — no connection to you — just a figure of speech."

She gave me a hard look, her eyes glinting in the moonlight. "You killed those people. From the news, it sounds like they had it coming."

I steered the boat and let the silence hang. She snuggled up against me. I didn't want to lie to her, but I wasn't going to discuss my work with her, either.

"I like you, Finn. I'm glad you're not working for O'Hanlon. You remind me of my brother."

"That's not exactly music to my ears. I had in mind a different kind of relationship between us."

She elbowed me in the ribs, hard enough to make me flinch. "You know what I meant. That was a compliment."

"If you say so."

"He's killed people," she said. "Not that he ever talked about it, but I could tell from the way he reacted to certain things. Threats, for example."

"You're okay with that?" I asked.

"Some folks just need killin', as they say in Texas," she said. "If he knew O'Hanlon was trying to snatch me, he'd go after him in a heartbeat."

"He doesn't know?"

"I haven't told him. He's not in any shape to go after these people. I don't want him to know; it could get him killed."

"I thought you said he was active in MMA. Doesn't sound like he's exactly a wilting violet."

"Physically, no. But not all his wounds were physical."

I wondered about that. PTSD? I decided to let it go, for now. "You're not in touch with him, then?"

"Not about this. Why?"

"I was hoping he could shed some light on why O'Hanlon was after you."

"What difference does that make to you?"

"I've decided I want on your team, Mary Beth."

"That's sweet, Finn. But you don't even know me. Not really.

I'm not some damsel in distress. I got myself into this; I can handle it."

"I don't doubt that for a minute. I'm not trying to be your knight in shining armor, to extend your metaphor."

"Then I don't get it, Finn. What's in it for you? Your best interests would be served by getting as far from me as possible."

"Except for one thing," I said, chewing on my lower lip.

"What one thing?"

"I'd miss you too much. I want to keep you around." I held my breath, waiting.

After several seconds of silence, the moon broke through the clouds and I got a look at her face. She was staring into the distance, tears rolling down her cheeks. She caught me looking and rubbed them away, forcing a smile as she locked eyes with me.

"I didn't mean for this to happen, Finn."

"I never thought you did. Neither did I, but here we are."

"I wish things were different," she said.

"They will be. Just wait."

"What do you mean?" she asked.

"Things change. If you don't like the way they are right now, just hang in there. Pretty soon, they'll be different."

"I'm not good at waiting patiently when somebody's chasing me," she said.

"No, I didn't figure you were. That's one of the things that makes us alike. Let me in, and let's kick some ass together. Then we'll see where we go next."

"I don't ... I'm not in a position to make any commitments, Finn. If I were, I'd latch onto you in a heartbeat and never let go."

"Yeah, I get that. That's all I needed to hear. I'm in."

"What's that mean?" she asked.

"It means you and I have things to do."

She looked up at me. "Okay, but first, I need to tell you some stuff about me and O'Hanlon. I didn't tell you the whole truth a little while ago. I'm sorry. I should have, but it's become a habit not to trust anybody."

I nodded. "Okay. I understand why you'd feel that way. I'm not pushing you to tell me anything."

"I know. You're so sweet to me. I know you're not going to do me any harm, but about helping me... Let me tell you everything. Then we'll see if you still feel the same way."

I wrapped my arm around her shoulders and gave her a squeeze. "Tell me. Then we can work out a plan for the next few days, at least."

She nodded and said, "It started when I found my parents. I didn't freak out like I told you. I had a pretty good idea what they were up to all along. Before I took off, I gathered up a few things they had stashed. Computer files, some notebooks, that kind of thing. They tried to keep me in the dark, but you know how nosy kids can be."

"And that's what O'Hanlon's after?" I asked.

"It's not that simple. I'll tell you, but it's going to take a while, okay?"

"We've got plenty of time."

17

ISLAND GIRL WAS SWINGING TO HER ANCHOR. WE WERE TUCKED well up inside Chatham Bay, Union Island, and the boat's motion was gentle. On a normal night, it would have put me right to sleep. But that night my eyes were wide open.

Mary Beth and I were stretched out on the V-berth. Her head was on my shoulder, and she was sound asleep. I was too busy processing what she told me over the last hour of our trip.

Now I understood why O'Hanlon was chasing her. He had $15 million worth of reasons. Her father was O'Hanlon's bagman, and Mary Beth walked away with all the codes for the offshore bank accounts after she found her slain parents.

She emptied the accounts before O'Hanlon knew what was going on, moving the money to her own offshore hiding places. I pressed her on how a kid like her had that sort of know-how, but she just said, "Remember, Finn, I grew up in that environment. It doesn't take a genius; it just takes someone who's paying attention to the details."

Not only did she steal the money; she also took her father's records of all O'Hanlon's suppliers and distributors. By now, they were a bit out of date, but from what she told me, they could put O'Hanlon in prison for a long time. And one file listed politicians who were on O'Hanlon's payroll. Several of them were prominent nationally. They had their own worries about where those records might be.

She wasn't sure if O'Hanlon or one of his rivals killed her folks. O'Hanlon accused her father of skimming; she overheard some harsh exchanges that summer while she was home. She believed it was a rival, though. O'Hanlon would have extracted the money and records from her father's grasp before killing him, by her reckoning. I agreed.

O'Hanlon at first assumed Mary Beth's brother was behind the theft. No college girl would have been savvy enough to do what she did, in O'Hanlon's view. His people were shadowing her on the college campus, all right. And he told her brother that if he didn't cough up the money and the records, Mary Beth would pay.

The brother responded by eliminating O'Hanlon's thugs, just as Mary Beth told me. Then O'Hanlon sent two of his goons to question her brother. They caught him in his gym, but cops responding to the neighbors' reports of screaming interrupted them. The goons were in bad shape by the time the cops got there. Her brother did them some permanent damage, but nobody wanted to press charges.

Before things turned ugly at the gym, the brother protested that he knew nothing about money and records. Based on that and the brother's handling of his interrogators, O'Hanlon shifted his attention to Mary Beth. He figured her for a softer target.

Besides, O'Hanlon got his hands on the police reports from the parents' murders. The only fingerprints found at the scene belonged to the parents and Mary Beth. That included the prints on a concealed safe, which was found open and empty. By the time O'Hanlon learned this, Mary Beth was on the run.

She also confessed that Mary Elizabeth O'Brien wasn't her

real name. Mary Beth told me that when I offered to get her a passport in a different name. Protesting that we didn't have time, she said she knew what that took. She spent months establishing her O'Brien identity, she said.

I knew a quicker way. After a series of encrypted text messages sent via my sat phone, I got a commitment for delivery of a new passport the next afternoon. We would wait for it in the anchorage between Petit St. Vincent and Petite Martinique.

"But they'll need a picture, at least," she'd said.

"They'll use the picture from the Mary Elizabeth O'Brien passport," I said, "assuming the U.S. passport office indeed issued it."

"They issued it all right, but they don't have my passport. It's here. How can — "

"Don't ask," I said, laughing at the look on her face. "I can't tell you how, but they have internal access to passport office records."

"Who are those people?"

"What people?"

"The ones you were texting," she said.

"Not sure which texts you mean," I said, unlocking the sat phone and handing it to her. "Show me."

She took the phone and scrolled through the menus, shaking her head. "There are no texts in the phone. How did... I didn't see you erase them. And there aren't any numbers in the directory or the caller ID folders."

"Yeah, I know. That phone never has worked right."

"You work for some government agency, don't you?"

"Me?" I raised my eyebrows. "Not me. I'm retired."

"Retired from where? You've never said."

"You never asked. From the Army."

She wrinkled her brow and shook her head. "I don't believe you."

I shrugged. "What can I say?"

"Finn?"

"Yeah?"

"Are you working for somebody like the FBI? Did they send you after me?"

"Nobody sent me after you, Mary Beth. You came to me, remember?"

She thought about that for several seconds. "Why are you doing this?"

"I told you. I like you — a lot."

"Is Finn your real name?"

"Yeah."

"First or last?"

"Last."

"What's your first name?"

"I've spent my whole life pretending I don't have one. My parents were flower-child druggies. I think they named me after a hallucination or something. Let it go, please?"

"I'll tell you my real name," she said.

"Not now. It'll just add to the confusion."

"What do you mean?"

"By this time tomorrow, I'll be trying to forget you were Mary Elizabeth O'Brien. You'll be somebody else."

"What about my credit cards? They're in the O'Brien name."

"There'll be new ones to match the passport. Don't worry about it."

"But the address, and the bank information for the automatic payments, and — "

"There'll be a one-time-use web address that lets you fill all that in."

"But what will I put for my home address? I shouldn't use the same one I've been using."

"No. There'll be a choice of several mail-forwarding services for you to pick from. And they'll all show up as bona fide residence addresses, if somebody checks the postal service database. Quit worrying about it."

"So we'll clear out from Union Island using my old passport?"

"That's right."

"And clear into Grenada with the new one?"

"I'm thinking that might not be a good idea," I said.

"Because somebody could connect the two identities from the outbound clearance from Union Island?"

"That's possible. They could also connect you to me, and just guess that the two identities belong to the same woman."

"What are we going to do, then? Petite Martinique is part of Grenada, right? We'll have to clear in there if we stay anchored there."

"Technically, yes. But Petite Martinique's a no-man's land. It's been a smuggler's haven since way back in the colonial days. Nobody will bother us if we sit there for a day or two. Especially if we don't go ashore."

"But then what, Finn? Like you said, we have to go ashore sometime."

"Yeah. We'll get your new papers and leave."

"But how does that help? There's still your passport, and the ship's papers."

"I have others. We'll sail north, up to Guadeloupe or Martinique. The French are pretty laid back. And we'll tell them we left from the U.S.V.I. and sailed straight there."

"You've lost me, Finn."

"We're on a U.S. flagged vessel. If we left from a U.S. port, they won't expect us to have outbound clearance papers. It's not required. We'll sort of be born again with our new identities once we check into one of the French islands."

She frowned for a couple of seconds, then laughed that laugh I loved to hear. "So, Finn whoever and Mary Elizabeth

O'Brien sailed away from Union Island on a boat named *Island Girl* and just disappeared?"

"It happens," I said. "This can be a dangerous part of the world. Boats disappear sometimes — storms, pirates, what have you."

By then, we were anchored, and we went to bed. She fell asleep at once, leaving me to ponder the conflicting stories she told me.

18

———

I WAS SIPPING A BEER AT THE TABLE IN THE MAIN CABIN, WATCHING Mary Beth — oops! Mary Helen Maloney, she is now — working to commit her new life's history to memory. We were anchored in shallow water on the eastern edge of the coral heads a mile and a half west of the channel between Petit St. Vincent and Petite Martinique.

The water was flat, protected by the reefs and islands in the distance. There was a brisk breeze across the deck, and the nearest boats were over a mile away, anchored within a few hundred yards of Petite Martinique.

We were all alone out here, which was the reason I chose the spot. An unlighted speedboat came by a couple of hours after sunset last night to deliver the package we were expecting.

"Most yachts don't anchor so far out here," the man at the helm said, waving as he passed a few yards from us at idle speed.

"There are lobsters among the coral heads." I gave him a casual wave in return.

At that, he tossed a package onto *Island Girl's* side deck and went on his way, speeding up as he gained some distance.

"You recognized one another?" Mary asked.

"Prearranged challenge and response phrases," I said, stretching across the cockpit coaming to reach the package. I tore it open and took out the passport, handing it to her as I flipped through the rest of the contents.

"Mary Helen Maloney. Can't shake that Irish ancestry," she said. "Why did they use Mary again? I expected a completely different name."

"Mary's a common enough name. If a first name's at all unusual, it's best to change it. But that can cause trouble. With a name that's common enough not to attract attention, it's better to stay with it. Or something close."

"Why?" she asked.

"It's harder than you think to get accustomed to answering to a different name, especially if you change identities often. Somebody could trip you up by using your old name. Besides, I'm used to calling you Mary, so I won't stumble over using a new name."

"But you've been calling me Mary Beth."

"Yeah, but I called you Mary for almost as long before you told me to call you Mary Beth. Why'd you decide to do that if it was an assumed name to begin with?"

She shrugged. "I had a friend named Mary Beth once. I always liked the sound of it. And it gave you a kind of... I don't know... special name for me? Something nobody else ever called me. Silly, huh?"

I smiled. "Sweet. I'm flattered."

"Good. I meant for you to be. I've gotten attached to you, Finn." She returned the smile. "Are you going to call me Mary? Or Mary Helen?"

"Unless you've got a strong preference, I vote for Mary."

"I don't care, but why Mary, just out of curiosity?"

"It's less distinctive; like I said, the more common an alias is, the safer."

"You've had experience doing this," she said.

I handed her the other papers and the two credit cards that had been in the package. "Your legend's in there. Read it over a few times while I get the computer online. And sign the backs of the cards and put them in your wallet. I'll need anything you've got that matches up with the Mary Elizabeth O'Brien identity."

"My legend?"

"Your background information, Ms. Maloney. Parents, childhood homes, schools, all that stuff. You need to commit it to memory and then we'll destroy the written version." I went below and took my laptop out of the drawer below the chart table.

She followed me into the main cabin, looking down at the papers in her hand. "What if somebody checks up on this stuff? Like, calls the high school, or something?"

"They'll get a confirmation of the information in your legend. And I'll get a warning that somebody's snooping."

"This is almost scary, Finn."

"Good."

"Why is that good?"

"Because it's deadly serious. Don't screw it up, okay? I'm hung out a little way on this, so take care of me. Don't blow it."

"Could you get in trouble for doing this?"

"Yeah, I could. But don't worry. Just take it seriously. We'll do fine."

"Why are you taking this kind of risk for me?"

"Same reason you wanted me to call you by a special name. I want to take care of you." I cleared my throat. "I'm not good at this man/woman stuff. I'm out of practice with the words."

"Thanks, Finn," she said, her eyes tearing up. "You're doing fine. I know what you want to say. Me too. We'll get there."

"I'm already there. Now get to work while I get an internet connection set up."

"Okay, but isn't that dangerous? Using public Wi-Fi? Where's it coming from? Petite Martinique?"

"It's probably coming from Carriacou. That's the big island right to our west. It can be dangerous, but I've got special software and I'll be connecting to that website through a VPN. It's secure. Don't worry about it. Now read the instructions about the credit cards and your address, okay?"

She nodded, and in a couple of minutes, she said, "Okay, I'm ready to fill out everything."

I handed her the open laptop and went back to the galley. I fished a cold beer out of the icebox and sat down across the main cabin from her while she worked on the computer at the dining table.

After about thirty minutes, she closed the laptop and looked up at me, smiling that smile. "All done. I can't believe it was that easy. I went through hell for months to become Mary Elizabeth O'Brien. How did they make this happen so fast?"

"I don't know, Mary. But don't worry. It's solid."

"What about you?"

"What about me?"

"Your passport and the ship's papers. They weren't in the package."

"I already have them."

"Oh. They're hidden somewhere?"

"That's right. I'll retrieve them once we're well away from land tomorrow. Just in case we get stopped by somebody like customs as we're leaving, it would be better to stick with the old stuff. It all matches our outbound clearance, including the vessel name on the transom."

"I was going to ask about that. It's painted on, isn't it?"

"Vinyl transfer lettering. It can be peeled off, if you're determined enough. I have two extra names with the papers. Once we're far enough out to sea, we'll heave to long enough for me to peel off the old one and stick on a new one. Then I'll break out the new paperwork and stash our old stuff."

"Where's your stash?"

"*Island Girl* has encapsulated ballast." I saw her frown, so I decided to explain. "Some boats have a ballast keel that's bolted onto the bottom of the hull. But others have a hollow keel that's filled with lead or something else heavy."

She nodded. "Right, I know about that. It's in the keel?"

"That's right. There's a strongbox epoxied to the top of the ballast casting. If you look down in the bilge, you'll only see smooth, painted fiberglass."

Now she frowned. "I looked, remember? Before we left Puerto Real, I pulled up the carpet and opened the sump. I don't recall seeing anything that looked like it could be moved, or opened."

I nodded. "You're right. There's a half inch of solid fiberglass down there, right over the top of the cavity with the strongbox."

"How do you open it?"

"With a power saw. Then I glass over it again and touch up the paint."

"That sounds like a lot of trouble."

"It's worth it if somebody searches the boat. It'll only take me an hour to do it."

"What else is in there?"

"Some money. A little gold."

"No weapons?"

I shook my head. "No weapons."

"I'm surprised. Why not?"

"Bad people usually come equipped with weapons. It's always better to use their own against them. Much less complicated to clean up afterward."

"Aren't you giving them a big advantage?" she asked.

"They think so. That works against them, most of the time.

You killed that woman in Bequia, and she was the one with the weapon."

"I see what you mean. I'd never really thought about that before. But I got the drop on her."

"There are all kinds of ways to get the drop on somebody. Even if they're armed and watching you. Sometimes that's almost easier, because they're cocky."

She nodded. "I see; that news report about the murders in St. Vincent is making more sense, now."

I nodded. "Forget about the murders in St. Vincent. We should get out of here early in the morning. Let's get some rest."

19

IT WAS LATE AFTERNOON, AND WE WERE ROLLING ALONG ON A NICE beam reach, making five and a half knots. Our course was roughly north, but we were just letting *Carib Princess* follow the wind. We left the anchorage at Petite Martinique around three this morning, taking up a broad reach until we were 20 miles to the west of the Grenadines.

That put us well out of sight of land by sunup, and there were no other boats nearby. There was no reason for anybody to be out where we were. The islands and reefs that made up the Grenadines were smoothing out the ocean swell that rolled in from Africa, so we hove to.

While Mary fixed breakfast, I cut into the bilge sump with my power saw. I collected one of my spare passports and another Coast Guard Certificate of Documentation, as well as a roll of waxed paper that held *Island Girl's* new name. Putting our old passports in the strongbox along with the *Island Girl* Certificate of Documentation, I closed everything back up.

By then, Mary had breakfast ready, so I stopped to eat with her before I repaired the fiberglass. Paint would have to wait until the epoxy cured, but that was okay. The bilge was grimy enough to keep my surgery from being too obvious unless somebody knew to look for it.

Mary squared away the galley while I blew up the inflatable dinghy. Securing it close against the transom, I climbed down into it and used a razor blade scraper to remove *Island Girl's* name. Too bad. I liked that name. Maybe I'd use it again, but for now, I had my own island girl. She was sitting in the cockpit, handing me the things I needed.

A few rags and some acetone cleaned up the transom well enough. Following my instructions, Mary unrolled the new name, turning it face down on the cockpit seat and smoothing it as best she could. She freed a corner of the backing with her fingernail and peeled a little of it away.

"That's good enough," I said. "Now take it by the two ends and hand it down to me. Once I've got it positioned, you hold it in place and I'll pull the backing out from behind it."

In another five minutes, I squeegeed the bubbles out of the lettering, and *Island Girl* was transformed into *Carib Princess.* Mary helped me stow the dinghy, and we cast off the back-winded jib, sheeting it in on the other tack. The jib filled, and the boat surged forward. Once we gained enough momentum, we came about. We trimmed the sails then, coming up on the wind until we were on a northerly course. We didn't need to go any farther to the west, for sure.

I leaned back on the windward side of the cockpit and hooked my left leg over the tiller. *Carib Princess* was happy on a beam reach; she didn't require much steering. Mary settled back next to me, pulling my right arm over her shoulders.

"I like it here, Finn."

"It's a pretty morning," I said.

"Yes. But that's not what I meant. I like snuggling up against you and feeling your arm around me."

"Good. Then I like it here, too."

"You didn't tell me your new name," she said.

"Finn."

"But that's your old name."

"Yeah, it was. It was my last name, but now it's a nickname."

"Will you tell me what your new name is? Or do I have to sneak a look at the ship's papers?"

"Did you?"

"Did I what?"

"Sneak a look at the ship's papers before, to find out my first name?"

"No. I wouldn't have done that. I knew it would embarrass you. But you don't have much of a stake in your new name, do you?"

"Nope. It's just one of many that I've used."

"You've used it before?"

"Nope. That's not usually a good idea. But I've used variations on the theme. This time, it's Jerome Edward Finnegan."

"I like it. Another good Irish name. Maybe I'll call you Jerry."

"Don't. Somebody might confuse me with my father."

"Your father? His last name wasn't Finn?"

"Get with the program, Ms. Maloney. I have a legend, too."

"You've already memorized it?"

"Memory's a learned skill. You can get pretty quick at memorizing things like that. Comes in handy in certain lines of work."

"I see. So, who were they? Your parents, from the legend."

"Mary Katherine and Jerome Edward Finnegan, from Dublin."

"They were FBI, huh?"

"What?" I asked.

She laughed that laugh. "Gotcha, didn't I?"

"I don't get it, Mary."

"That's okay. If you're from hard-core Irish Catholic stock, FBI means foreign-born Irish. Like from the old country."

"I've never heard that," I said. "But anyway, they weren't."

"You said they were from Dublin."

"Dublin, Georgia. Hicks from way out in the country. No close neighbors when they were growing up. Makes it tough for anybody to check up on them. Besides, they're both dead now."

We spent a few minutes watching two frigate birds keeping pace with us off our port side. They got bored and moved on, and Mary broke the spell.

"Where are we going, Finn? Martinique or Guadeloupe?"

"Either's fine for our purpose. We can start anew in either place. Martinique's closer by maybe 70 miles. It would take us around 15 hours longer to get to Guadeloupe."

"How long to Martinique, then?"

"It's roughly 100, maybe 115 miles from here. If the wind holds, we'll get in tomorrow morning around breakfast time."

"We can't just keep doing this?"

"Sure we can. As long as you want."

"Right now, I'd be happy just to keep sailing forever."

"Well, we ought to clear into Martinique and establish our new identities. It wouldn't be as easy to clear into most other countries without papers from our last port of call. We could do it, but it would call attention to us. We don't need that."

"Okay, spoilsport. Martinique it is, then. What's it like?"

"It's a great place to hang out. Huge island, half a million people. It's part of France, so you find all kinds of stuff from the E.U., from groceries to designer clothes. Interesting history, nice museums. Great restaurants. Or you can avoid all of that and enjoy the same laid back, simple life that the other islands offer. You speak French, by any chance?"

"Not so you'd notice. Just a few phrases. I took it in high school. You?"

"A little. It's not necessary, but a lot of people there don't speak much English, which makes it fun. It's one of the places where yachties hang out for months at a time. The living is good, and it's easy. Easy to lose yourself there, too. There aren't that many Americans. That's another attraction, given our situation."

"How do you mean that?" she asked, frowning.

"O'Hanlon's thugs would stick out like whores at Sunday school."

She was quiet for several seconds, then she said, "I can't keep hiding for the rest of my life. At some point, I'll have to deal with those bastards."

"Yeah, that's what I figured. When you're ready, I'm here to help, but we need to regroup and figure out how you want to deal with them. Martinique's a good place to work our way through that."

"Why?"

"Partly because it's France. It has much tighter ties with Europe than with the U.S."

"Okay, but why does that matter? I mean, given my problems."

"The guy who brought your passport?"

"What about him?"

"He came from Martinique."

"You said you didn't know him."

"I don't. But I know that. His boat had French registration numbers, and the prefix was from Martinique. And your passport likely came from a U.S. embassy in Europe, based on my experience. In a diplomatic pouch on a direct flight."

"I see. Tell me more about that, would you?"

"I can't."

"Can't? Or won't?"

"Can't. I don't know details of how that works. In my line of work, everything's compartmentalized. Need to know. And I never needed to know that."

"In your line of work? But you said you were retired. From the Army."

"And that's true. I am retired from the Army."

"Finn?"

"Yes?"

"You've swept me right off my feet. I'll go wherever you take me. Sorry about all the questions, but your air of mystery is like catnip to me."

"Okay. Well, now that I've swept you off your feet, I'm going to take you to Martinique. Then we can figure out what the next step in solving your problem is."

"Thanks. If we're sailing overnight, I'll go sack out for a few hours. Might as well stand four-hour watches, huh?"

"Sure," I said. "Rest well."

She stood up and leaned down to give me a kiss before she went below. "Something to remember me by until we meet again," she said.

20

Taking my big, beat-up straw hat from the port cockpit locker, I pulled it down on my head. The sun was up now, and my skin didn't need more sun damage. I was already a poster child for skin cancer. I took a sip from my bottle of water and thought about what I was mixed up in.

I was besotted with Mary, and she as good as said she felt the same way about me. Neither of us used that four-letter word, though. Not yet. Me, because it always messed things up when they were otherwise going all right. I suspected her reasons were similar. At least I hoped so. I trusted my judgment of people most of the time, but I didn't have much recent experience with young women in love. We'd see how things played out.

I was glad she said she couldn't just keep running. She was keeping her feet planted in reality, no matter where her heart was. That was good. O'Hanlon's people went to a lot of trouble to find her in Bequia. I didn't buy her first story about Puerto Rico and crewing on *Sisyphus,* even before she changed it. It could have been true, but it was flawed enough to make me question it.

Big yachts were businesslike when it came to hiring crew. They would have passed on recruiting somebody with no more experience than she had. The story about the abuse by the male crew members wasn't far-fetched, though. She could have been a target of opportunity for a bunch of jerks without adult supervision. I was relieved when she told me it was all bullshit.

The latest version of her story, the one about being kidnapped by O'Hanlon, made a little more sense. But there were still holes in it. She said they snatched her in Miami and sailed to Fajardo. I wondered why they waited until they got to Fajardo to try forcing her to hand over the money and the files. It would have made more sense to work her over in mid-ocean, where they were less likely to get caught.

I didn't press her on that, but I didn't think she told me the whole story. I understood; given what she went through, it was tough to trust anybody. On top of that, she saw me do several suspicious things. She needed a little time to get used to the idea that I was on her side before I started asking hard questions.

The three men who'd tried to snatch her in Puerto Real could have been muscle for somebody like O'Hanlon. They fit the profile, and it would have been simple enough for them to track her to Puerto Rico, however she really got there.

My working assumption was that O'Hanlon did own *Sisyphus*. He might have even been aboard, waiting to have her brought to him. But the real questions were how Mary came to be in Puerto Rico, and what she'd been doing there.

It seemed more likely that she got there on her own, not that someone took her there against her will. If I were in O'Hanlon's position and I snatched her in Miami, I would have gotten her as far away from U.S. soil as I could. They would have gone right past all those uninhabited islands in the Bahamas to get to Puerto Rico. Anywhere would have made more sense for kidnappers with a victim aboard than Puerto Rico or the U.S.V.I.

There were other parts of her story that didn't quite ring true. This whole business with her brother, for example. The more she talked about him, the fuzzier the story became. For example, if he was her savior and protector, why wouldn't she have told him about stealing O'Hanlon's money and files? And then there was the story of the goons attacking him at his gym.

If he'd already killed two of their pals, they wouldn't have let him get the upper hand. And they would have picked somewhere private to question him. They wouldn't have tried to jump him in a place where the neighbors could overhear and call the cops.

I was curious about why he was estranged from their parents. He must have had some contact with them, otherwise, how would he have become close to Mary, given the difference in their ages?

I took another swallow from my water bottle and tried to rein in my thoughts. There were all kinds of reasons why Mary might not be telling me everything. After all, she went through at least two violent encounters at the hands of whoever was after her. She also noticed there were things about me that were a little off, as well. I could hardly blame her for keeping her guard up when I was doing the same thing. I just happened to have a little more practice at it.

Then there was the possibility that she didn't have a good handle on her situation. For all her self-assurance, she didn't have all that much experience to draw on. She was doubtless confused about certain aspects of her plight; anybody in her position would be.

All that aside, there was a strong and growing bond between us. I was alive because I was a shrewd judge of people. I might be a little out of date on courtship rituals, but I didn't doubt that our feelings for one another were the real thing.

That was enough for me, at least for now. I learned long ago to take life minute by minute. She was enjoying my company, and I was enjoying hers. I would hang on to that and count my blessings.

The rest would work out, one way or another. No one could know what would happen to us, but I intended to make sure that whatever it was didn't happen at the hands of this O'Hanlon character. Once we got to Martinique, I would find the time to do a little background work on him.

My client kept track of who was who in the realm of organized crime. That kind of information came in handy in my line of work. People like O'Hanlon often became either our targets or the scapegoats for some of the things we did.

While I was researching O'Hanlon, I would check up on Mary's parents and her brother, too. That reminded me; I should find out what her last name was before she took up the Mary Elizabeth O'Brien identity. I would have to find a way to ask her about that before we got to Martinique.

I would feel her out on what she planned to do about O'Hanlon, too. No doubt she was thinking about that. I knew what I would do in her situation. There was only one way I could think of to stop a guy like that.

When your only tool's a hammer, all problems look like nails. I was a hammer user from way back, and my experience over the years only reinforced the notion that, as Mary said the other day, "Some folks just need killin'." The world would be a better place without O'Hanlon, in my reckoning. I'm sure Mary shared that view.

There could be problems with that, though. Guys like O'Hanlon were hard to kill. They got to the top of the heap by being shrewd and ruthless. It was a safe bet that O'Hanlon wouldn't be a pushover. And sometimes people like him have partners who would want revenge — family, often as not.

Mary had O'Hanlon's business records, somewhere. I

wondered if they were aboard. If they were and we could deci-
pher them, we might discover whether somebody was
watching O'Hanlon's back. Depending on how well-connected
he was, the repercussions for executing him could be
significant.

We might piss off some powerful people, not necessarily all
in the drug business. O'Hanlon got his hands on the police
reports of her parents' murders. According to Mary, that's how
he ended up on her trail. His ability to get those records said
something about his connections.

Thinking of records made me wonder again where she hid
the ones she stole. She mentioned computer files, but her
father might have had paper records, too. And what did she
have in mind doing with them? Their value as leverage
decreased over time.

There was a lot of turnover in the drug business; if the
records were a few years out of date, they might be harmless.
Given that Mary was sharp enough to have taken them, though,
she probably knew that.

I wasn't doing well at reining in my thoughts. Needing a
little distraction, I decided to go below and plot our position.
Maybe throw together a peanut butter sandwich. I lashed the
tiller and stood up, stretching the kinks out of my back.

By the time I got a GPS fix and marked the chart, Mary
stuck her head over the lee-cloth. When she saw me, she
climbed out of the makeshift berth that was also the starboard
settee.

"What's up, Finn?"

"Just plotting a fix, for something to do."

"How's our progress?"

"Great. We're rocking along, averaging five and a half knots.
You get a nap?"

"Slept like a baby. Time for a watch change?"

"It's only been three hours," I said.

"That's okay. I'm good, if you want to stretch out."

"Don't mind if I do. Thanks."

She squeezed past me and gave me a little kiss on her way to the companionway ladder.

"Take my hat," I said, handing it to her. "Sun's brutal out there."

She smiled as she grasped the brim. "Thanks. Get some rest."

She put the hat on the chart table and pulled her hair back into a ponytail, fastening it with a rubber band she took from around her wrist. Picking up the hat, she settled it on her head, gave me another smile, and disappeared up the ladder.

21

"That was a real treat, Finn," Mary said, as I rejoined her in the cockpit. We traded watches through the night, and I just finished cleaning up the galley after cooking and serving breakfast.

"Glad it hit the spot," I said, pouring us each mugs of coffee from the thermos. I handed her one and sat down beside her as she steered with her foot on the tiller.

"I didn't even know you could eat flying fish," she said.

"Nature's bounty. We sailed through a school of them last night, and I guess they were running from predators. They kept bouncing off the boat, anyhow. I picked up half a dozen nice ones off the deck, after the first one hit me in the face. I was almost asleep when the little rascal smacked me."

"Well, they were a great side dish with the eggs. Even better than bacon."

"Healthier, too, I'm told. I'm glad you enjoyed them."

Close-hauled on the starboard tack, *Carib Princess* put her shoulder into the chop. We watched the sun rise as we passed Diamond Rock; we were on course for Ste. Anne, Martinique.

We would have the anchor down in a few hours. We planned to spend the afternoon recovering from our overnight sail. Taking the dinghy into Le Marin to check in with customs and immigration could wait until the next morning.

"I'm still amused by a comment you made the other day," I said, taking a sip of my coffee.

"What comment was that?"

"Calling people born in Ireland 'FBI.'" I chuckled. "Foreign-born Irish. It's so... I don't know... not quite bigoted. Provincial, maybe. The notion that Americans of Irish descent are the 'real' Irish is what fascinates me about it. People born in Ireland wouldn't consider themselves foreign-born; they'd think you were foreign-born. I don't quite have a word for that sort of twisted logic."

"So, you've never heard that before?"

"Not until you used it, no. Was it common where you grew up?"

"Yes, I guess. When I was little, we had a parish priest who came from Ireland. I heard my dad refer to him as FBI in a conversation with one of his friends. It had a derogatory tone to it, but I didn't pick that up at the time. I was old enough to know what the FBI was, so I thought that's what Dad meant."

"I can see why that would be. It confused me, and I'm not a little kid. How'd you figure it out?"

"Asked my mother. She said, 'Oh, it's those damned billy-goat Irish your father sprung from. Those Daileys, they're nothin' but potato Irish.'"

Bingo! I thought. *Her family name is Dailey, and I didn't even have to ask.* I wanted to be sure, though. "Dailey? That was your father's last name?"

"Francis X. Dailey," she said.

"X? For Xavier?" I asked.

"Of course, for Xavier." She laughed. "Finn?"

"What?"

"You weren't raised as an Irish Catholic, were you?"

"Nope. Methodist, and before you ask, I have no idea."

"No idea about what?"

"Where the name 'Finn' came from. I mean, how far back, how many generations. I know it's Irish, originally, but that didn't mean anything in my family. It was just a name, like Smith or Jones."

"Okay," she said. "Sorry I jumped to the wrong conclusion about you. It was just the way things were when I was growing up. Kind of us and them. You would have been one of *them*, for sure."

"No harm done. But you used two other terms I'm curious about."

"Which ones?"

"Billy-goat Irish and potato Irish. They're derogatory?"

"Yes. They're applied to the people who left Ireland during and after the famine, usually by people who consider themselves to be *lace-curtain* Irish."

"The lace-curtain Irish were better off?" I asked, with a laugh.

"Well, they thought of themselves as a better class of people. Not necessarily richer, but better educated, more refined. Richer was part of it, but my mother's family didn't approve of my father, even though he was a wealthy man by the time they married. 'Married down, your mother did,' my aunt told me, any time she got the chance."

I wanted to ask her what her mother's maiden name had been, but I decided not to press my luck. It would come out later. If not, I had enough background on her family to find it on my own, now. "Did that bother you? What your aunt said, I mean."

"No. I was just a kid. You know how stuff goes over your head when you're little."

"Yeah. Like a lot of the stuff that was drilled into me in Sunday school. When I was little, I just accepted it at face value. Then I got older, and I began to see that some of it didn't square with the way the church people acted."

"You still consider yourself Methodist?"

"No, not really. I don't think about religion much. I just let everybody believe what they're comfortable with. How about you? You still a practicing Catholic?"

She chuckled and shook her head. "I'm not what the Church would call practicing. But when you're immersed in it from birth, like I was, that whole culture is part of you. There's not much you can do about it. It's something you're stuck with — like your eye color or something."

We drank our coffee and sailed along in silence for several minutes. That was one of the best things about her. She didn't feel compelled to fill the silence. We were both comfortable with it. I didn't know many people who were that way.

"Hey, Finn?"

"Yeah?"

"You said there was good shopping in Martinique."

"There is. Looking for something in particular?"

"I could use some clothes. In case you haven't noticed, my wardrobe's limited to a pair of ragged cutoffs and two T-shirts. And a bikini."

"Shouldn't be a problem. You can find basic stuff right in the marina near the customs and immigration office. Even a few upscale places. But you can get anything you want — designer labels from all over the world, in Fort-de-France."

"Basic stuff's what I had in mind. But I wouldn't mind seeing Fort-de-France. You said there were museums there. Is it far?"

"Not too far. There are buses. Or we can go anchor right in the heart of town, but that's in the midst of all the commercial shipping traffic. Not as quiet and pretty as where we're headed right now. We could move around there later, though, if you want."

"Let's play it by ear. Buses are okay. I cheated a little and looked at the guidebook in the chart table. I like the sound of Ste. Anne. I could stand a few days to just chill out, if it's okay with you."

"It's better than okay; it's why I live this way. Chilling out's what I do best. We'll square the boat away and head into the marina. You can scout the shops while I clear us in. Have you got a cellphone, by the way?"

"No, just the one I took away from the woman in Bequia. Why?"

"We should get you one, so we can stay in touch if we split up ashore. They're easy enough to come by. You still have the one you took from her or did you ditch it with the pistol?"

"I still have it. I took the SIM card out, though. I've heard that's better, to keep anybody from tracking it."

"Yeah, but it's not foolproof. Even if you put another SIM card in it, the phone's got unique codes hard-wired in. Somebody that knows what they're doing can find it if it's powered on, even without a SIM."

"What should I do with it, then? I kept it in case I wanted to eavesdrop on their texts again, but those guys know by now that the woman's dead. Should I toss it over the side?"

"Yes, but first make a note of those names and phone numbers in the directory, would you? I'll take my laptop in when we go. While you're shopping, I'll see if I can find out anything about those people. O'Hanlon, too. Jot down whatever you've got on him along with the stuff from that phone."

"I'll go do that now, okay?"

"Sure. There's a little spiral-bound notebook in the chart table. Just rip out however much paper you need. We're probably an hour from dropping the hook, if you want to take a nap, but I figured we could crash for the rest of the day once we got anchored. Time enough for customs and immigration clearance in the morning."

"Sounds good to me. I'll go make the notes while I'm thinking of it, though."

She gave me a kiss on the cheek and picked up our empty coffee mugs on her way below.

Mary left me at the entrance to the marina restaurant the next morning. Our inbound clearance only took a few minutes; we were first in line when the customs and immigration office opened. The restaurant was only a few steps from there.

I sat down at a secluded table and ordered an espresso. The waitress gave me the access code for the restaurant's Wi-Fi network, and I settled in to see what I could find out about Mary's parents and O'Hanlon.

I struck out on the names from the cellphone Mary took from the woman she killed in Bequia before tackling Mary's family. The results of my search for Francis X. Dailey were overwhelming. I would never get through it all before Mary finished her shopping.

I flagged down the waitress and ordered a second espresso. While I waited for it, I scrolled through the list of articles on the screen of my laptop, scanning them.

I glanced at the time in the upper right-hand corner of the screen. Mary only left a few minutes ago. I offered to buy her a cup of coffee before she left, warning her the shops might not be open this early, but she'd been undaunted.

"Then I'll just window-shop until they are," she said. "You said you had stuff to do online, so don't worry about me. I can amuse myself in a place like this for hours with no problem."

"Well, okay. Why don't you pick up a phone, first thing? The places that sell phones might open before the clothing stores, anyway."

"Good idea," she said. "I'll call you once I do that, so you'll have my number. Or better yet, I'll send you a text. That way I won't interrupt what you're doing. I'll try to stay out of your way until lunchtime, okay?"

"If that suits you. It's no big deal; I just need to catch up on email and a little financial stuff. Maybe read the news from home. Whenever you get back will be fine. I'll be here."

When the waitress brought my espresso, I did a second search on F. X. Dailey. This time, I included the word 'murder' to narrow the results.

Time permitting, I might go back and pick through the articles in the society columns. Mary's parents were part of the South Florida social scene; my initial search filled the first page without a single article about the killings.

This time, I still found an overwhelming number of articles, but these were all related to the Dailey's deaths. I scrolled through several pages and went back to one of the earlier ones dealing with the double murder.

Dailey was a property developer; he cut a wide swath through Florida over a period of several years and apparently made a lot of money. He and his wife were killed in their 10,000-square-foot beachfront mansion.

There were no pictures of the bodies, but the description of the crime scene by the housekeeper who found them didn't leave much to the imagination. As Mary said, they were butchered.

The speculation in the first article I read was that the motive was robbery. Mrs. Dailey was known for her expensive jewelry, and it was all missing.

The housekeeper said Mrs. Dailey kept it in a safe in the master bedroom suite where she found the bodies. The safe was open and empty. The obvious conclusion was that the Daileys were tortured to extract the combination.

The article suggested that this pointed to someone who knew that Mrs. Dailey kept her jewelry at home. The police weren't saying much at that stage. They were canvassing the neighborhood and asking anyone who was in touch with either of the victims during the previous few days to call them.

Time of death was not yet established, according to the article. Pending results of an autopsy, the medical examiner's comment was that the Daileys appeared to have been dead for at least a day before the bodies were found.

The article went on to describe the neighborhood and other recent burglaries in the area. I skipped through the next several articles, skimming for new information and moving on.

A couple of weeks after the discovery of the bodies, the articles decreased in frequency. There was a dearth of facts, at least as reported by the news sources. Given the prominence of the victims, that told me the trail was cold.

To my surprise, there was no mention of a surviving daughter in any of the articles. The Dailey's son, Francis Xavier Dailey, Jr., who lived in the suburbs of Atlanta, declined to talk to the press. He was mentioned in several of the articles, but where was Mary?

I flagged down the waitress and ordered another espresso. When it arrived, I closed the laptop and slugged down the rich, bitter coffee. That was one more reason I liked the French islands. As I savored the caffeine rush, I wondered who Mary was.

Did she think I wouldn't discover the flaw in her story? I

couldn't accept that; she was too smart to make that kind of mistake. She must have figured I would catch on eventually.

She volunteered Dailey's name; she must have thought I would check on the murder. And if she wasn't Dailey's daughter, how did she fit into this whole puzzle?

My musing was interrupted by a ping from my iPhone. I glanced down at the screen to see a text message from a number with a Martinique country code. The next three digits, 696, marked it as a mobile number. I pressed my index finger to the home button, unlocking the phone and bringing up the messaging app.

"Hi, Finn. Got a phone. Lots of interesting shops. A couple open already. See you around noon."

I responded, *"Glad you got a phone. Thanks for the update. Good hunting. I'll be here when you're done."*

I waited 30 seconds, and when there was no response, I put the phone down. Using the satellite phone, I could have fired off an encrypted text to one of my support contacts and asked for background on Mary. But I left it on the boat. With the info from her O'Brien passport, they could find things most people wouldn't believe. If she was in the system anywhere, they would find her.

Then it crossed my mind that they might already have done that. The contact I used for the passport owed me a personal favor; I called it in when I asked for a fresh identity for a new lady friend.

That didn't mean he wouldn't have checked her out while he was at it. That was the way these things worked. I didn't worry about that possibility at the time; I didn't have any reason not to trust what she told me.

I debated going back to the boat for the satellite phone, but I decided not to do that just yet. Whoever she was, Mary was no threat to me. Asking them to do a background check on her could open a whole different can of worms. If they already ran background on her and found something I should know about, they would have told me by now. I would wait and see what she was up to. I could always send that text later if necessary.

I opened the laptop again. Mary wasn't due back for two hours, at least.

A search for Rory O'Hanlon turned up over a hundred thousand hits in half a second. I clicked through the first half-dozen pages, but none of the results looked relevant. There were lots of Rory O'Hanlons. The people on the first few pages were in the public eye for various reasons: actors, musicians, writers, and so forth. None of them looked promising.

I scanned a few more pages. Then I started seeing ads for online services that offered to search public records, telephone directories, and voter rolls for a fee. They claimed to tell you everything you wanted to know about all the Rory O'Hanlons all over the U.S. I skipped that option.

I wasn't surprised that I didn't find the guy. The name was a common one, and successful mob bosses were good at avoiding publicity. The O'Hanlon I was looking for could be buried in the search results, but I didn't know enough about him to narrow the field.

I could ask my contacts to check out Rory O'Hanlon, but I wasn't in a hurry to do that. I already ran a small risk by getting a new identity for Mary. A background check on her wouldn't be too hard to explain.

I pictured the people sitting in a secure facility somewhere saying something like, "Well, old Finn's robbing the cradle, but at least she's good looking." They'd blow my fling off as some midlife crisis. They'd get a chuckle out of it. They might even tease me about it at some point, but nothing bad would come of it.

If I made a personal request for background on a mob boss, though, innocent explanations wouldn't be the first ones they would come up with. They would be more likely to think I was contemplating a freelance hit, or trying to settle a personal score.

People in my line of work have been known to do things like that. It wasn't taken lightly. Disciplinary action might follow, depending on O'Hanlon's situation. And there was only one type of disciplinary action that applied to people like me. It was terminal.

I was retired, but that didn't mean the same thing for people like me that it meant for ordinary government employees. They couldn't order me to carry out missions any more. I could decline assignments as long as I did it before I knew the target.

And that was about it as far as my being retired. I still got paid, plus a special bonus when I accepted a job.

Checking out a new love interest was one thing. It might be pushing the limits, but they would overlook that. Given all the secrets in my battered old head, they would think it was a prudent thing for me to do — and for them to help me with. Nobody wanted me to fall in with the wrong crowd. Going into business for myself with the government's resources was a different matter.

I closed the laptop. There was another option to learn about O'Hanlon. I could ask Mary. For that matter, I could ask her about the other stuff, too, but that might put her off. Asking her about O'Hanlon was different.

I already volunteered to help her deal with him, and while she didn't embrace the idea, she didn't reject it, either. She wouldn't think my asking about him was strange. I would just have to be careful about how much faith I put in her answers.

I looked around for the waitress, thinking another espresso would be nice. Then I saw Mary come through the door. I glanced at the time, surprised at how quickly the morning passed.

Mary was dazzling. I almost didn't recognize her. She wore

a simple dress, a sleeveless white sheath, with a Creole madras scarf tied around her waist. It set off her tan to a stunning degree. She spotted me gawking at her and laughed, walking toward the table with several shopping bags swinging from her left hand.

"Hi, sailor," she said, bending down to kiss my cheek. "Buy a hungry girl lunch?"

"Yes, ma'am! Sure thing." I got to my feet and pulled out a chair for her.

"Close your mouth, Finn." She giggled. "You'll attract flies." She sat down and shoved her bags under the table.

"You look beautiful. I almost didn't rec — "

She put her index finger over my lips. "Stop! You're about to mess up, silly."

"What?" My confusion must have overcome my normal poker face, because she giggled again.

"I know what you were about to say; you were going to spoil it."

"How? Spoil what?"

"I could tell by the look on your face."

"But I said you were beautiful," I said, wrinkling my brow.

"And that was fine. Thank you. But you were about to say you almost didn't recognize me."

"Oh."

"Yes. Oh, indeed. You're supposed to let me think I'm always beautiful. Saying you didn't recognize a girl because she was beautiful for a change could hurt her feelings."

"I'm sorry. I wasn't expecting you yet, and I... "

"Nice try at recovery, Finn. Can we get a quick lunch and go back to the boat? I'm tired. Besides, I want to model the rest of my clothes for you. That stunned look on your face was a serious boost to my ego. I could stand to see that again."

"But I blew it."

"I'm just messing with you. You didn't blow it. You were cute. What's good here?"

"Ever'sing here is ver' good, madame," the waitress said, walking up and handing us menus. "You like a carafe of zee house wine? Is a ver' nize sauvignon blanc."

I looked at Mary and she nodded, smiling.

"Yes, please," I said.

"I bring while you look at the menu, then."

23

"You like my new things?" Mary asked, after she'd modeled her purchases for me. We were back aboard the boat, sitting on the starboard settee with our legs stretched across the narrow cabin, our feet resting on the edge of the port settee. Mary was snuggled against me, her head on my shoulder, my right arm around her. I didn't know about her, but I was still exhausted from our sail.

"I do. I like them all," I said, "but the dress is my favorite. It makes you look like you stepped right off the cover of a fashion magazine."

"Aw, you're sweet, Finn. It was a pure impulse buy. That whole outfit was in the window of one of the touristy shops. I'm not sure what possessed me to buy it."

"It changes your whole look."

"Careful," she said, giving me a gentle elbow in the ribs. "I let you off the hook once already."

"You're always beautiful, but the dress was such a dramatic change," I said. "That's what I was trying to say when you cut me off in the restaurant."

"I knew what you meant, Finn. I just like to mess with you. Don't let me get to you."

"I wasn't expecting you to show up for lunch dressed like that. You'd said you were looking for basic stuff. I figured shorts and polo shirts you know. Like the rest of the things you got. Practical."

"Yeah," she said. "Me too. I'm not usually a girly girl, especially not when I'm living on a boat. But I saw the dress and thought it would be fun to wear it for you. Surprise you, like."

"It was fun for me," I said. "I hope my reaction was suitable."

"I could tell you liked it. The look on your face when you recognized me made my whole day."

She turned her face up and kissed my cheek. "Are you as tired as I am?"

"I'm beat," I said. "Ready for a nap."

"So am I. I forgot to ask, though. Did you get your business taken care of online?"

"Yeah, I did. Nothing big; just catching up."

"There's something I meant to tell you before we went ashore. Between the excitement of landfall and the exhaustion from our overnight trip, I just didn't get to it."

"What's that?" I asked.

"About me. I was going to tell you when I came clean about my not really crewing on *Sisyphus* and the other stuff, but I got sidetracked."

"Tell me now?"

She nodded and scrunched her face into a frown. "Well, I told you the Daileys were my parents."

"You did, yes." Poker face in place, I kept my tone even.

"They were, in a way. But they weren't my biological parents."

I raised my eyebrows. "Not your biological parents? You were adopted?" I was curious to see what she'd do with that opening.

"No, not adopted. I met them not long after I started college. I grew up dirt-poor. My mother was a single parent, and she was a... " Mary shook her head. A few seconds passed.

"Anyway, I worked hard in high school; I figured an education would let me break free from my past. I got a partial scholarship to college, but I stopped and worked every other quarter to make ends meet. I was majoring in business, and I got a job as a paid intern in the Dailey's development company."

She looked at me, and I nodded. "I see."

"Their legitimate business," she said. "They were successful developers — condos, golf courses, retirement communities, you name it. Both of them were involved in it. I started with them right after the first quarter of my freshman year. I worked my ass off to make myself indispensable, and they sort of took me in. They helped me pay for college; they wanted me to keep working with them when I finished, and I liked that idea. It worked out. I finished my degree and went to work with them full-time. The whole thing was like a dream come true.

"Their business was an ideal setup for laundering money. I figured out what was going on pretty quickly. Lots of cash flow, to and from all kinds of off-the-wall people and businesses. They kept me out of that, but it was a pretty small operation, given their volume of business. I could see what they were up to, but I kept my mouth shut. No way was I going to screw up a good thing. I knew what the other kind of life was like."

"Okay," I said. "Thanks for telling me."

"I don't want to keep secrets from you, Finn. You're the only person who's ever given me any help, except the Daileys."

"What about the brother, then?"

"I was an only child, and my mother died when I was in my senior year of high school. But the Daileys did have a son. He lives in Atlanta. He really was estranged from them. I met him once, not long after I started with them, but that's about it."

"Is he a veteran?"

"Yes. And he's into mixed martial arts. He tracked me down when I took off after I found their bodies, like I told you. But we didn't hit it off. He knew about me, knew I wasn't mixed up in their off-the-books businesses. He told me that O'Hanlon was probably behind his parents' murders, and that I should be careful.

"He took me back to Atlanta and let me stay in his extra room until I got my wits about me. He said if I needed anything, I could call on him. Seemed like a nice enough guy. And O'Hanlon's thugs did go after him later on because they thought he took the money and the records."

"Where'd you learn to fight? Did he teach you?"

"No. I picked that up the hard way, on the streets, when I was a kid. The neighborhood I grew up in was gang turf. I did what I had to to survive; I'd rather not talk about that right now, though."

"Sure, that's fine."

"The Daileys owned a sailboat, a thirty-footer. They lived in a mansion on the beach, and they kept the boat in a little private marina close to their home. It was on the back side of the barrier island, on the Intracoastal Waterway. They let me live on the boat to help me save money. They offered their guest house to me, but that was more than I could accept. The boat was one thing; living rent-free at their mansion was something else. I looked after the boat for them. They didn't use it anyway, and they were paying a maintenance service to keep it up. I took care of it, and they saved money. I felt okay about that; like I was earning my keep. That's how I learned to sail. I made up the story about my dad racing Lightnings."

"Okay," I said, stifling a yawn. "And the Folkboat, too?"

"Yes, that too." She sighed. "I feel better, now that I've come clean with you. I'm sorry I wasn't honest with you to begin with."

"You had to get to know me. I understand that. Don't give it another thought."

She smiled. "Thanks, Finn. I feel that nap coming on, now, big-time."

She gave me another kiss on the cheek and moved to the port settee, stretching out on it. She was asleep in a minute or two, leaving me to ponder what she told me.

She was smart as hell. Street smart, for sure, but there was more to her than that. She figured I was snooping on her past while I was online. I didn't know how much of her latest story was true, but she touched all the bases I knew about, anyhow.

There were still things about the Daileys' son that didn't add up. Like why he bothered to track her down after his parents' murders, for example. And what made O'Hanlon think the son took the money and the records?

Then there was the whole story about her time with the Daileys. I wondered how many other people worked for them. I knew developers often didn't have a lot of employees, but judging from the publicity the Daileys got, I didn't see them as a three-person shop. What happened to the other employees?

I forced myself to come to grips with my real, deep-down, central question. What the hell was I doing here? With Mary, I mean. I didn't survive all these years without learning to question my motives every so often.

I was lonely and a little bored with this retirement thing. I got enough jobs to keep me from going 'round the bend, but I still spent more time alone than was healthy. Mary was a nice distraction for me; I wanted to keep this relationship going, but part of me realized I was pathetic.

I was objective; I knew what I was. For my age, I was an attractive enough specimen. I was fit; I still had all my teeth and most of my hair. I could be personable when it suited me; I could mix and mingle with people.

But what did I offer Mary? She wasn't much older than my

daughter. I could tell she liked me, but I knew I was just a fling for her. Given that she stumbled onto me, I could see why she would hang on. I was useful to her at the moment.

For whatever reason, she was on the run. I was cover and company, and I was no slouch in a fight. But I still felt a nagging worry about her showing up in my life.

I'm skeptical of coincidence. What were the odds of Mary's finding somebody like me right when I could do her the most good? This wasn't the first time I plowed this particular ground, but with what I just learned about her, I needed to work it some more.

There were lots of variations, but I only saw three options to explain her presence. She could be on the run — that is, she was what she said she was. People on the run often didn't tell a coherent story about themselves. That was option one. She could be working for the same people I worked for, here to check up on me. That was option two. Or, she could work for an unknown enemy who wanted to pick my brain. That was option three. It helped to boil it down that way.

There were three explanations for Mary's being here. I worked through them before, but I still needed to figure out which one applied.

She might be a plant, sent by my former employer to check up on me. Did I do something that caused them to send someone like Mary to check me out?

I couldn't think of anything. Besides, while Mary fit the pattern of one of our agents in some ways, there were things that made her unlikely in that role.

For one, she killed that woman in Bequia. Or did she? Thinking about that, I realized that she *told* me she killed the woman in Bequia. There was no independent verification. That whole scene could have been staged. So could the one in Puerto Real, for that matter.

She could also be working for someone else, someone who

knew enough about me to arrange our encounter. I'm not a valuable target in my own right, but somebody might want to leverage what I know. Some of my targets over the years were well-known. Our enemies could harvest a wealth of propaganda if they could extract what was in my memory. It was possible that Mary was bait.

I didn't like admitting it to myself, but the more I thought about it, the more probable it seemed that Mary was a plant. I already knew she wasn't what she appeared to be. If she worked for my employer, then I would play along and see where we ended up. But if she were working for anybody else, I'd have to do away with her.

I didn't like that idea; I was far too attached to her for my own good. I needed to work out a rationale for her presence in my life.

If she was sent here, I knew what to do. In one case, I would play along; in the other, I would take her out in deep water and do away with her.

Or, if she were indeed on the run, I needed to know who was chasing her. I would help her if she were a victim of the mob. But it occurred to me that I didn't have any verification that she was on the run from a mobster named O'Hanlon -- nothing except her word.

She could be a crook herself, in which case I was less inclined to side with her. That wasn't an absolute, though. In my view of the world, there are degrees of evil. Good and bad run together most of the time.

What I needed to do was establish whether O'Hanlon was real. That might not be his name, but it would do for a place holder — and whether he was after Mary. If those two things were true, I could eliminate the other two explanations for her presence.

Once I ruled out the other two explanations, my choices

would depend on how the relative merits of Mary's game balanced against those of her enemy's game.

My grasp of the situation was better now; I needed to find out about this O'Hanlon character, and I could start with what Mary knew. She should have every reason to level with me about him. If he didn't exist, well... I'd miss her when she was gone — either back to my employers or to the briny deep. She would be out of my life either way.

I hoped that she was telling me the truth, at least in a macro sense. I was seriously attached to her. But she said it herself; I would do what my survival required.

Having solved all the puzzles I could solve without more information, I swung my legs up onto the starboard settee and stretched out for my own nap. As I was dropping off, I took a last look at Mary. She was sleeping peacefully. I hoped that meant she was what she said she was.

24

"Hey, Mary, did the cops ever figure out who killed the Daileys?"

She took a sip of wine to wash down the cheese and cracker she was finishing. We were having refreshments after our naps.

"Not that I know of. They grilled me and Frankie pretty thoroughly, but — "

"Frankie?" I asked.

"Their son. He's Francis X., Junior. Anyway, I don't guess they saw either of us as suspects after they got through with us. The murders were big news for several weeks, and then it all went quiet."

I nodded and took a sip of my wine. We were in the cockpit, in the shade of a tarp lashed over the boom. We were sitting on either side of the companionway, leaning against the coachroof, facing aft.

The cheese and crackers were on a platter on the bridge deck between us. We were in a perfect spot to enjoy what promised to be an outstanding sunset. I didn't want to spoil the magic, but I needed to ask a few more questions.

I put down my wine and picked up a cracker. Mary was watching me, waiting, inviting me to continue.

"Didn't the cops think it was suspicious that you took off running instead of reporting the bodies?"

"Yes, at first. It didn't help that my prints were on the safe where Mrs. Dailey kept her jewelry, either."

"You mentioned that before. You said it was open and empty when the cops got there. Does that mean you emptied it after you found them?"

"Yes. It was hidden. Whoever killed them didn't know about it, I guess."

"Was there anything that might have indicated the killer searched the house?"

"No. Not when I found them."

"Why did you open the safe?"

She picked up a cracker and nibbled at a corner, her eyes fixed on the cheese platter for several seconds. She looked at me, her face drawn, her eyes beginning to tear up.

"Look, Finn. I am what I am. I never got a break until I met the Daileys. They were the first good thing that ever happened to me. I was devastated when I found them dead, but my reaction was like, 'Oh, shit! End of the gravy train. What am I going to do now? No job, living on a boat I don't own and couldn't afford, student loans to pay.' I freaked out, all right. Like I told you, but not for any reasons I'm proud of. I fell back on my survival skills from childhood."

"And you knew about the safe?"

"Yes. It was behind the mirror over her dresser. You had to know how to swing the mirror aside. It had this trick catch, and it was hinged, but it looked like it was permanently fastened to the wall."

"How did you know the safe was there?"

"She liked to show off her jewelry, and she treated me like

her daughter when I let her. She let me wear some of it, for these business-related social events we'd have to attend."

"Did you go in and out of the safe much? You knew the combination, I take it."

"Yes, and yes. She gave me the combination. Sometimes when we were going from the office to a social function, she'd send me to the house to get a piece of jewelry out of the safe for her. Or for myself, if she suggested it."

"Did it occur to you to wipe your prints off the safe?"

She nodded. "But their absence might have been suspicious, so I decided not to. I worked for her, remember? My prints were all over the place — their house and the office — and other people knew she loaned me her jewelry sometimes."

"She must have really trusted you," I said.

"She did. And I trusted them. I wouldn't have done anything to hurt her. Or him. She was a nice lady. Frank was a great guy, too. Not what you'd expect from big-time crooks. They were good to me, just out of kindness. They never asked for anything in return. I figured they were trying to fill the hole left by their son by taking me in."

"Did you ever learn why they were estranged from him?"

"He told me. They never discussed what went wrong, but I asked him. He figured out they were crooked sometime in his teens. He was a straight arrow, boy-scout type of guy. He ran away and joined the Army as soon as he was old enough. Cut them off completely."

"You said the records and the money were in the safe. Had you seen them before you found the bodies?"

"No. They were in two of those metal document boxes in the back of the safe. I knew the boxes were in there, but she told me they were personal papers, deeds, stock certificates, that sort of thing." Mary shrugged. "After I found them dead, I took everything. I suspected that they were laundering money for somebody. I told you that, already."

"You never told anybody you took the stuff out of the safe?"

"Nobody but you. Once I found out what I had, I knew it would be worth my life if it got back to O'Hanlon."

"Yeah, I can see that. Seems he found out anyway."

"From the police report. It mentioned my fingerprints on the safe."

"How do you know that?"

"From the men on *Sisyphus*. They told me. They said I could save myself a lot of pain if I handed it all over before O'Hanlon got rough with me."

"Did you ever meet him?"

"I was never introduced. I knew when he was around, but the Daileys kept me away from him, like they were ashamed of him, sort of. He came to their house — never to the office. They'd always tell me they needed private time with him, and I'd get lost."

"You said you overheard an argument they had with him."

"Yes, I did. Not long before I found them. I couldn't hear everything, but I picked up that he was accusing them of skimming."

"What do you know about him?"

"I think I've told you everything I know about him. He's from Boston; some kind of Irish Mafia big shot. I looked through enough of the files to get a feel for what he was into, which was just about anything crooked that you can imagine. And he has some well-known politicians on his payroll."

"What did you do with the stuff you took? You emptied the offshore accounts, but what about the jewelry and the files?"

"They're in safe deposit boxes. I spread them around. Different banks in different cities, under my O'Brien name."

"Thought about what you're going to do with them? I mean the records, in particular."

"No. I wish I'd never touched them, now. O'Hanlon's people

on *Sisyphus* said he might be willing to cut a deal with me — trade the money for those files."

"What do you think about that?"

"I think it was bullshit. People like that don't make deals with somebody like me. Or they for sure don't honor them."

"If you could be sure they'd honor their deal, would you do it?" That was a test for her. I was curious to see her reaction.

She gave me a hard look, those pale gray eyes cold as ice. "No way. They kill people, Finn."

I was searching for how to respond, but she shook her head and kept talking.

"I know what you're thinking. I killed that guy on *Sisyphus*, and the woman in Bequia. I didn't have much choice. It was them or me. O'Hanlon and his bunch are cold. They only care about making money. They don't give a shit who gets hurt."

I nodded. She was right. I didn't point out that it was her own greed that got her into this. But I knew what she would say. She already laid the groundwork.

"Suppose you could call your fairy godmother and get her to sort this out for you. How would it end?"

"Don't, Finn. You know enough about me by now to know I don't have a fairy godmother. I only see two ways for this to end."

"Yeah? What are they?"

"One is with me dead. I don't like that one."

"And the other one?" I asked. "That has to be with O'Hanlon dead, I guess."

"I wish it could be that easy," she said, "but it's not."

"You don't really think killing a guy like him would be easy, do you?" I asked.

"No, but even if that could be done, there will always be another asshole like him, or worse. You know how these people work. Somebody's already waiting in the wings to take his place."

"So that's not your second outcome?"

"No. It's probably a necessary step, but it's not the end game."

"So, what is the end game?"

"I don't know yet. I'm still working on that. You got any ideas?"

"I'm still working on it, too. I'll let you know if I come up with something."

"Please do; I feel like I'm running out of time."

"We've got time, Mary." I poured a little more wine in our glasses. "Let's forget O'Hanlon and watch the sunset. Then we've got the whole evening ahead of us. We'll have a nice dinner in Ste. Anne. And after that, one of us will think of something."

"Thanks, Finn. If I had a life, I'd spend it with you."

"Yeah, I know. I feel the same way. We'll work things out. Now, watch the sunset. We may get a green flash."

25

I SAT IN THE COCKPIT IN THE COOL OF THE EVENING, ENVYING Mary's ability to drop off to sleep as soon as she closed her eyes.

After she told me about taking the Daileys' files, we went ashore for an early dinner in Ste. Anne. Both still exhausted from the overnight trip, we came back to the boat and went to bed. Mary was snoring softly seconds after her head hit the pillow.

I wasn't so lucky. I tossed and turned for a while trying to make sense of all the different stories Mary told me since we left Puerto Rico. After half an hour, I gave up. I poured myself a drink and took it up to the cockpit.

This young woman was playing me. I needed to hold onto that thought. I might be falling in love with her, but I couldn't let my feelings obscure the fact that she was manipulating me.

Her confession this afternoon rang true, but then so did some of the other tales she told me. The woman was smart, and she was an accomplished liar.

I dealt with plenty of less than truthful people over the years. Most of them had a tell, a quirk that gave them away once you learned what to look for. A change in the facial muscles, a blink, something. If Mary had one, I wasn't able to spot it.

She confessed that lying was a survival skill for her. As much as I wanted to, I couldn't afford to trust her. Before I could weigh the risk of sticking with her, I needed to know what she was up to.

I resisted the urge to construct a scenario to explain her behavior. My judgment was impaired by my emotional attachment. As seductive as it was, coming up with a rationale for her lying would have been too easy.

I wanted more information on the Daileys and O'Hanlon. My only source so far was Mary, and she wasn't reliable.

Some people I've run across had distorted perceptions of reality. They spun convincing tales as readily as Mary did. The shrinks said they believed their own lies. Several of my targets over the years possessed that trait.

Mary's ability to lie so credibly was worrisome. I needed solid reference points before I could figure out how to deal with her. A background check on her might help. So far, I resisted the urge to order one.

I was hesitant because I already found enough red flags to worry me. I was afraid of what the report might reveal. I was happier than I remembered being in a long time, thanks to Mary.

Discovering that she presented an unacceptable risk would be hard to take. Keeping my head buried in the sand was a more appealing option. If she were a threat, I didn't want to know.

Besides, I reminded myself, my client probably checked her out when I asked for the passport a few days ago. They might not have been as thorough as they would be if I told them I planned to marry her, but they would have done a basic check. If they found anything too damning, I would have gotten a text by now.

Who was I kidding? I wanted to keep her around. I began to focus on what I needed to know to keep us both safe. She told me several things that weren't consistent with one another.

The Daileys' estranged son was a puzzling element. Mary at first said he was her brother, and that he helped her pick up the pieces of her life after the Daileys' deaths.

Then she confessed that she was not a blood relative of the Daileys, but she still claimed Frankie found her when she ran away. That was a consistent part of both versions of her story. He took her in and gave her a place to stay.

Yet she said they didn't hit it off, she and Frankie. There was something off about that.

Why would he appear out of nowhere to help Mary? He was estranged from his parents and had no relationship with Mary, according to her. And why would he have let her stay in his home?

She said the police grilled both of them. That wasn't surprising. They would have both been prime suspects in the killings, either separately or together.

Then there was O'Hanlon, hot on Mary's trail. Or was he? I didn't have independent verification of that. She said O'Hanlon was after her, but...

While I didn't know if the O'Hanlon threat was real, somebody was trying to capture her. I saw plenty of evidence of that. So far, I didn't have a reason to doubt her on the topic of the Daileys' mob connections. Whether they were tied to O'Hanlon or some other mob boss didn't matter right now. I would just stick with the name O'Hanlon, even if it was only a placeholder.

I was intrigued that O'Hanlon went after Frankie Dailey, Jr., before he shifted his attention to Mary. If Frankie cut his ties to his parents because of their criminal activities why would O'Hanlon have thought Frankie would take their money and files?

Mary's fingerprints on the safe made her the more likely thief, and they explained why O'Hanlon's people were chasing her. He must not have learned about her fingerprints until later in the game. That might have taken the heat off Frankie.

I couldn't believe O'Hanlon's thugs left Frankie alone, though. Not after they tried to interrogate him. That was out of character for mobsters. Once they tangled with him, they wouldn't have walked away, especially if he kicked their asses. There was more to that story than Mary had told me.

If the news reports were right, the Daileys were dead for at least a day before their housekeeper found their bodies. She found them in the early morning when she went to work.

If Mary found them the day before and cleaned out the safe, that gave her at least a 24-hour head start before the housekeeper called the cops.

She said Frankie found her in Alabama. Driving that distance from South Florida in 24 hours was possible. But why would Frankie even have been looking for her?

He wouldn't have heard about his parents until after the housekeeper found them. Then he would have had to track Mary down. The timing of his involvement didn't fit.

How would he have found her? How long would it have taken? And why did he care about finding her? Had he really given her shelter and helped her get on her feet again? Why would he have done that? She said they didn't hit it off.

I lifted my drink to my lips and discovered it was empty. I thought about having another, but decided against it. My head hurt already. Lack of sleep, alcohol, or too many confusing thoughts? It didn't matter. I needed sleep. I was worn out, finally.

I went below and put the glass in the galley sink. Rather than risk disturbing Mary by climbing into the V-berth with her, I stretched out on the starboard settee.

In the morning, I would ask her more about Frankie and

O'Hanlon. Maybe I would take my laptop to the marina restaurant and use their Wi-Fi to do a little more research. This time, I would take my satellite phone in case I changed my mind about that background check.

I would have to find a way to distract her. There was always shopping. She said she hardly scratched the surface of the shops in Marin.

26

I woke up to the smell of fresh coffee. As I sat up and swung my feet to the floor, Mary handed me a steaming mug and gave me a peck on the cheek.

"You slept on the settee. Rough night?" she asked.

"I couldn't get to sleep."

"Too keyed up?" she asked.

"Trying to make sense of this mess you're in."

"I'm so sorry, Finn. I didn't mean to drag you into this."

"You didn't drag me in; I invited myself. And I'm not sorry about it, so don't you be. I just don't understand what's going on."

"Can I help? Is something specific bothering you?"

I took a swallow of coffee to buy myself a little time. After a few seconds, I decided to ask her about Frankie. Worst case, she would just spin me another yarn.

"Frankie Dailey," I said.

"What about him?"

"You said he was estranged from his parents."

"Yes. That was the way they described their relationship."

"They? The Daileys?"

"Yes. Why?" she asked, frowning.

"If they were estranged, why would O'Hanlon think they'd stashed their records with Frankie?"

"I never thought about that," she said. "Do you suppose it was a ruse?"

"A ruse?" I wasn't sure where she was headed.

"By the Daileys, I mean. You think they were pretending to be estranged from him as cover? Like to protect him?"

"That's a possibility, I guess," I said, "but you're the one who knew all of them. What do you think?"

She put two fingers on her chin and tilted her head. After a few seconds, she said, "I need some of that coffee." Stepping back to the stove, she poured herself a cup.

She came back into the saloon and sat down across from me, taking a sip of the coffee. "I never thought about it. Now that you mention it, though, maybe it was."

"Maybe it was what?" I asked.

"A ruse," she said. "That would make sense, wouldn't it? If he was working in their business, I mean. I guess I was too involved to see that. Clever insight on your part."

She was doing it. I almost didn't catch it; she was the one who suggested the idea of a ruse. Now she was giving me credit for it. Two could play this game.

"Thanks," I said. "I thought of it last night. It was probably more obvious to me because of my distance from the situation."

"That gives you perspective," she said, nodding. "Did you think of anything else that wasn't quite right?"

I took a swallow of coffee and debated with myself. I could ask why Frankie tracked her down. Or how he even knew she was on the run. I settled on a more direct approach.

"How well did you know him?"

"Frankie?" she asked, raising the mug to her lips.

Now that I was watching, I could almost see the wheels

turning in her head. I nodded and brought my own mug to my lips. I nodded. "Right, Frankie."

"Not well. I only met him the one time, like I told you."

Oh, yeah? I thought. *What about when he let you stay at his place in Atlanta while you were on the run?*

"That was at the Daileys," she said, "right after he came back from one of his tours in Iraq. I hadn't been working for them long at that point. But I picked up bits and pieces from them over the years."

"About his military service?"

"Right. And the mixed martial arts stuff. All of it. Looking back on it, they seemed proud of him. I guess the ill feeling was on his side, not theirs, huh? If he really was estranged. But I'll bet you're right. That was probably a smokescreen, that business about being estranged."

She's reinforcing the idea that I came up with the notion of a ruse. Damned clever, I thought. "You mentioned that he was wounded in Iraq."

"That's what they said. But he was okay; he wasn't permanently disabled or anything."

"You said he was discharged from the Army with a disability pension."

"That's right. I think he had mental problems, like PTSD or something. That's why he couldn't fight in the MMA matches anymore."

"I see," I said, taking another gulp of coffee. "That would explain his losing control, maybe."

"Losing control?" She raised her eyebrows.

"You said he tried to kill a couple of his cage-fighting opponents."

"Oh, right. That's probably it."

"There's something else I was wondering about," I said.

"What's that?"

"Still about Frankie. You said he came and found you when you flipped out after you found the Daileys."

She frowned and drank some coffee, looking down and to the right. "That's right. He did. I was pretty much out of it, Finn. Hysterical, I guess. I don't know what else to call it. I couldn't focus on anything — no idea where I was, what to do... I guess I did meet him more than once, but..."

She shook her head and looked up at me, her lips pursed, her brows knit. "I've never been like that, before or since. I think it must have been what they call a fugue state. I had no sense of time passing, or anything."

I waited, letting the silence drag out. I was wondering if she would elaborate on the inconsistency between this and her claim a few minutes ago that she only met him once, at his parents' house.

"Funny how I said I'd only met him the one time. I guess I blanked that out, the time at his place in Atlanta. I can't remember much about that, about him coming to get me. Or the time I spent at his place. I guess I was in shock."

But you were sharp enough to transfer $15 million and hide all their records, I thought. *She was as slippery as a snake, slithering out of that lie.*

"Did you ever wonder how he knew?"

"How he knew?" she asked, frowning. "The news, I guess. You mean about his parents? It was all over the news."

Not until you'd been on the run for 24 hours. Guess your fugue state could have hidden that little disconnect from you. Nice advance excuse for inconsistent memories, I thought. "How he knew you were on the run," I said. "That's what I was getting at."

She shook her head. "I never thought about it. Maybe from the police?"

"From the police?"

"They would have notified him of his parents' deaths, right?"

"Yes," I said. *But he would have had to track you down and then travel to wherever he thought you were.* "I'm sure they would have. You think they told him you were missing?"

"I don't know. They must have."

"How do you suppose he found you? It didn't take him long, did it?"

She took a sip of coffee, giving herself a little time. "You're right. I was so shaken up I never thought about that. How could he have known where to look?"

"How long had you been on the run when he found you?"

"I remember driving through the night, but it's all run together. I can't say if it was one night, or more than one." She shook her head and pursed her lips. "Like I said, a fugue state."

"You said you didn't have any cash when you took off." *Let's see where you go with that.*

"Right. Maybe a few dollars. Not enough to buy more than a few fast-food meals. When I tried to buy gas, none of my credit cards would work."

"That's odd," I said. "Why do you suppose the cards didn't work? More than one card?"

"Yes. I had two; they were company credit cards. I didn't have cards of my own, back then. I guess somebody must have frozen them." Mary was frowning.

Before the bodies were discovered, I thought. "Who managed the company credit cards?"

"I did, normally. But either of the Daileys could, too. Or maybe there was some other problem with the accounts. I don't know; my mind was foggy. Maybe I messed up entering the zip code on the gas pump or something."

"Did Frankie have access to those card accounts?"

She stared at me for several seconds. "Not that I knew of, but..."

"But?" I asked.

"Well, you've got me thinking. If he wasn't really estranged from his parents... That could have all been a scheme they had to hide his involvement from O'Hanlon."

She's off and running now. This new story is all based on 'my' idea that the Daileys' strained relationship with Frankie was a ruse. "Why would he have frozen the cards, though?" I asked.

She shook her head and stared into space for several seconds. "Suppose Frankie was... No, that's too far-fetched."

"Tell me. It may seem different if you say it out loud."

She looked me in the eye and nodded. "If Frankie was working with them under the table, could he have had something to do with their deaths?"

"What makes you think that?"

"It fits," she said. "It would explain how he knew to start looking for me before the bodies were found, and maybe even how he found me so fast."

She's quick. She spotted that inconsistency, and she's explaining it away before I can ask about it. With that kind of creative ability, she should write crime novels. "I'm not following you on that."

She smiled. "You've helped me make sense of all that, Finn. If he was secretly working with his parents and was in on their murders, it all fits together. He might have even known before they were killed — certainly before the housekeeper found them. That's why he was looking for me, probably. If he had access to the credit card accounts, he could have tracked me down that way."

"But why would he have turned on his parents?" I asked. *How will you play off that one?*

"I told you O'Hanlon accused them of skimming. Maybe he was using Frankie to spy on them. If Frankie was working for O'Hanlon... See the possibilities?"

I nodded. "All kinds of possibilities. You think Frankie knew about the murders in advance, is that it?"

"Well, it sure looks that way, now that you got me thinking about it. I think you're right about that."

I'm right about that? She's doing it again. "You said Frankie took you to his place in Atlanta, let you hang out there for a while."

"That was while I was still dazed. I don't remember much about that. You're wondering why he would have done that?"

I nodded. "You said you barely knew him. It seems a little strange, especially if he was working for O'Hanlon."

She shrugged. "I don't know. Maybe he wanted to see how much I knew about the crooked part of their business."

"Did he ask you a lot of questions?"

"I don't remember. Like I said, I must have blanked it out. Maybe he drugged me. The first clear memory I have of the time after he found me is in Savannah. I was working as a barmaid in a place on River Street. How I got there from Atlanta is beyond me. I just don't know."

"A barmaid in Savannah?" I asked, not hiding my skepticism. "And how long did you do *that*?"

"Not long. Once I got my wits about me, I realized I needed to disappear before O'Hanlon figured out I'd ripped him off. Maybe a few days, that's all."

I nodded but didn't say anything. After a minute of silence, she asked what we were going to do today.

"I need to take care of a little business online. I figured you might want to finish checking out the shops in Marin."

"Sounds good to me. Think we could go to Fort-de-France tomorrow?"

"Sure. Or even after lunch," I said.

"Tomorrow. I'm still a little worn out from our all-night sail night before last. Let's just hang out this afternoon."

"Fine with me. Give me five minutes to shave and gather up my stuff," I said. "We can have breakfast at the marina restaurant. Then you can go shopping and I can use their Wi-Fi."

27

After we finished breakfast, Mary left to go shopping. I watched her walk out of the marina restaurant as I savored my espresso. Damn, I wanted to find a way this could work. Despite her lack of veracity, she was a hell of a woman.

The waitress brought our check, and I paid with a 20 euro note and told her to keep the change. I took my laptop out of the bag and set it on the table. While it booted up, I thought about what I wanted to do this morning.

Frankie Dailey was a big part of the puzzle. From his parents' obituary, it appeared that he was his parents' only surviving relative. Beyond that, all I knew about him was what Mary told me.

Her web of lies was troubling. I excused her deception earlier, but now it was beginning to bother me. She should trust me by now, at least a little. Was she so mixed up she couldn't tell fact from fiction?

The chiming of the laptop as it came to life saved me from fretting over that any more. I opened the web browser and typed "Francis X. Dailey, Jr." into the search box.

The first reference was a sponsored one, a link to the

webpage for his gym. I would come back to that. I skimmed a page worth of articles on his fighting career, including one that detailed the two fights that led to his suspension. Mary told the truth about that.

The first one led to a warning; Frankie continued to choke his opponent long after the man lost consciousness. It took two officials to tear him away. The second one was worse; he deliberately maimed the other fighter after knocking him out.

The second article mentioned his struggle with post-traumatic stress disorder. He did three tours in Iraq before his discharge, so his PTSD wasn't a big surprise

I scrolled back up the screen to the link to his webpage. There was a short bio there; it didn't tell me anything I didn't already know. The headshot of Frankie showed him to be ruggedly handsome, with a few scars around his eyebrows and a nose that was a little askew.

I clicked my way through two more pages of search results without finding anything else of interest. There was no mention of Frankie's life before he got out of the military. I was a bit surprised that I didn't get a link back to his parents' obituary. I guess even search engines miss something once in a while.

Aside from his MMA career, Frankie wasn't newsworthy. Nothing I found contradicted what Mary told me. That was comforting; she was finally starting to level with me.

And maybe she really was in a fugue state after she found the Daileys. Or on drugs, but we talked about drugs when we first met. She denied using them, and I believed her on that one. She showed no signs of having been a drug user.

She told me back when we first met that she was clean, and so far, she was. If she were using, I would have known it. Frankie could have drugged her without her knowing, though. I wouldn't hold that against her.

She even suggested that Frankie might have drugged her

when she was staying with him. That led me to comb through our conversation from earlier this morning.

She was smooth; I gave her that. I caught her twisting my words several times, once I was on the lookout for it. How many times did she do that earlier in our relationship?

I didn't know. At this point, I couldn't go back and look for other instances where she manipulated my understanding of her situation. We spent too much time together for me to analyze our exchanges with any objectivity.

Besides, I acknowledged to myself, I didn't want to know. She made me happy. Her life was rough; there was ample evidence of that. There were doubtless things she was hiding, things she was ashamed of.

We all had those. I surely did; I wasn't about to share my past with her, or anybody else. Why should she be different? She ran afoul of some dangerous people, and she did what she had to do. I wasn't trying to pry into her past for frivolous reasons; I only wanted to be sure she wasn't setting me up for something.

The more I watched her wriggle out of the traps created by her lies, the more I realized none of them were about me. She lied to me, all right, but not about anything that involved me. She was only trying to preserve her own dignity.

I already pried into her past more than I had any right to. I needed to stop; she wasn't a threat to me. I needed to leave her alone with her tangled past and focus on enjoying what we had. None of that history mattered; keeping her safe was the important thing.

Although I didn't want to keep nagging her, I did want to know more about O'Hanlon. I worked my way back through our discussions of him, looking for something that might let me narrow the scope of an online search.

And then it came to me. There was a loose thread I could pull. Mary's first memory after Frankie found her in Alabama and took her to his place was of working as a barmaid in Savannah. She couldn't recall how she got there.

Suppose Frankie worked for O'Hanlon and had prior knowledge of the Daileys' murders. He might have tracked down Mary because they thought she stole the money and the files. Frankie and O'Hanlon would have wanted those files even if they didn't have the Daileys killed.

There was no way to tell if Frankie or O'Hanlon knew about the safe in the Daileys' bedroom, but they knew Mary was close to Mrs. Dailey. Mary mentioned meeting Frankie at their house while she was working for the Daileys.

It would be surprising if a guy like O'Hanlon failed to check out a key employee of the Daileys, even though she was only involved in their legitimate business. Mary might not know much about him, but I would bet he knew a good bit about her.

The news reports mentioned the open safe and Mrs. Dailey's penchant for expensive jewelry and speculated that someone tortured the Daileys to make them hand over her jewels.

It wouldn't have been much of a leap for O'Hanlon and Frankie to connect the safe to the missing records. Given that Mrs. Dailey had let Mary wear her jewelry, they would have suspected Mary might know something she shouldn't. Plus, Mary said O'Hanlon's goons told her he knew from the police report that her fingerprints were on the safe.

Frankie could have snatched her and drugged her, keeping her in his place in Atlanta while they questioned her. Once they decided she was clean, they could have turned her loose while she was still dopey. If they'd been feeding her something like roofies while they questioned her, her memories would be scrambled.

She came to her senses in Savannah. There must be a reason she was there. Savannah was a four-hour drive from

Atlanta. Why would she have ended up there when they set her free?

On a whim, I typed O'Hanlon, Dailey, and Savannah into the search box of the web browser. I got several hits, but one caught my eye. There was an article in the Savannah paper about an Atlanta restaurateur named Rory O'Hanlon opening a place in an old warehouse on River Street.

I followed the trail back to Atlanta and discovered that O'Hanlon owned restaurants and nightclubs all over the southeast. The puzzle pieces began to fit together. I could almost feel them click into place when I saw that several of his clubs were in places developed by the Daileys.

Maybe there was more to Mary's tales than I thought. I was eager to share what I found with her; it might help her remember something useful.

I glanced at the time in the upper corner of the laptop screen. It was almost two p.m. Mary left to go shopping five hours ago. She planned to be back for lunch; she was late.

I took my cellphone out of my pocket and called her. After a few rings, I was forwarded to voicemail. The message informed me that the voicemail for her number was not set up yet.

Puzzled that she didn't answer, I tried again with the same result. I sent her a text reminding her that she was late for lunch and asking her to call me.

Walking around the shopping area to see if I could find her would be reasonable, but I didn't want to lug the laptop case around. I would drop it off at the boat and come back ashore. That would give her half an hour to get my message and respond.

If I didn't hear from her by the time I got back here, I would go looking for her.

28

As I tied off the dinghy and climbed aboard *Carib Princess* — I still thought of her as *Island Girl*, but I was working on it — I noticed that we forgot to put the drop boards in the companionway. That meant we failed to lock up, as well. Careless.

I climbed down the companionway ladder and dropped the laptop bag on the chart table. I sensed something wrong as I turned to face forward.

That's when I noticed that the bifold door that separated the forepeak from the main cabin was closed. I frowned; that was more odd than our forgetting to lock up.

Carib Princess is built to a design from the '70s; she doesn't have a lot of space below deck. That bifold door was intended as a concession to privacy, I guess, but it makes the boat seem claustrophobic. I knew we hadn't closed it.

Someone came aboard while we were ashore. I took a first step toward the bifold door and it snapped open. I froze.

"Good, Finnegan," Frankie Dailey said, the pistol in his right hand trained on me. "Don't make any sudden moves, okay?"

I recognized him from the headshot on his website. "Okay, Frankie."

Surprise flashed across his face, but he recovered quickly enough. He held our passports in his left hand. Reaching behind him, he put them on the V-berth, but his eyes never wavered from mine.

"Since we're using first names, do you go by Jerome, or Jerry?" he asked.

"Neither," I said. "Everybody calls me Finn."

"Finn," he said, nodding. "That your real name? Jerome Finnegan?"

"Why do you ask?"

"Just curious. I see Mary's changed hers."

I didn't say anything, and he smiled for a few seconds.

"I guess she told you about me," he said, breaking the silence.

"Not really."

"No?" he asked. "Then how'd you know who I am?"

"Oh, she mentioned your name, but she didn't seem to know much about you. I looked you up on the web, saw your picture on your website."

He nodded. "What did she tell you about me?"

"You were estranged from your parents, you did a tour as a sniper in Iraq, and you're into MMA."

"Uh-huh. And what did she tell you about herself?"

"She worked her way through college with some help from your parents, went to work for them full time when she graduated. Your mother kind of adopted her. When they didn't show up at the office one day, she let herself in their place and found their bodies. She freaked out and went on the run."

He grinned and shook his head. "What else?"

"She was broke and spaced out in Alabama, credit cards didn't work. She said you found her and helped her get her act together. Took her back to your place in Atlanta for a while so she could regroup."

He laughed at that.

"Why's that funny to you?" I asked.

"You have no clue, do you?"

I frowned. "About why you're here?"

That got another laugh. "About anything."

"Apparently not," I said. "Are you going to fill me in?"

A serious look came over his face. He studied me hard for several seconds, his eyes sweeping me from head to toes.

"Who are you?" he asked.

"We did that. You've got my passport. Jerome Finnegan."

"Yeah, yeah. Finn. But who are you?"

I shrugged. "What do you want to know?"

"Where'd you meet Mary, for starters?"

"Puerto Real, at the dinghy dock. She was looking to hitch a ride."

"Yeah? Your lucky day, huh?"

"I think so, yes."

"Where'd she want to go?"

"Anywhere but there."

"That was you, then?"

"What was me?"

"With her when my guys fucked up trying to grab her. You did that?"

"You should hire better help. All I did was steal the car keys. She kicked the shit out of your boys all by herself."

"You broke the driver's jaw."

"Good to know I haven't lost it."

"Yeah. That wasn't your first rodeo. My guys don't go down that easy. Taking down the driver blew your cover."

"How's that?"

"Mark of a pro. You know that. Gave you all the time in the world to deal with the others."

"She took care of them just fine without my help."

"Uh-huh. And in Bequia?"

"I don't know what happened there. I left her aboard and

caught the ferry to St. Vincent. That's where I was when your three morons blew that one. How'd you track us there, anyway?"

"We have local contacts there. You left there with one set of identities and checked in here with different passports. Different ship's document, too."

"How'd you find us here?"

"The *morons* in Bequia left a tracker on this tub. So she killed the woman?"

"Like I said, I wasn't there. It was all over by the time I got back."

"Look, Finn, I came out here to see who you were."

I nodded. "Okay. Satisfied now? My face matches my passport?"

He smirked. "I'm satisfied that you're a smart-ass of some kind. You give off all the wrong vibes."

"I'm so sorry you feel that way, Frankie."

"You're gonna be sorrier. You woulda been better off if you'd pissed your pants. You're way too cool about lookin' down the barrel of a pistol. I think you're gonna have to come with me. We need to get to know one another a little better so I can decide what to do with you."

"Where are we going?"

"Just to the marina."

"You have *Sisyphus* there? That where Mary is?"

"Not *Sisyphus*. Sailboats are too slow. I don't have the patience that Rory does. My boat's called *Aeolus*. Motor yacht."

"Yeah, okay. Makes sense. You strike me as a throttle jockey."

"Keep it up, wiseass. Your turn's coming, right after we get through with sweet little Mary."

"Then you *are* the son of a bitch who interfered with our lunch plans." I shook my head.

"Turn around, Finn."

I turned my back to him.

"When I give you the word, you climb the companionway ladder. Stop in the cockpit, and stand there facing aft until I tell you different. If you make a wrong move, I'll pop you in the elbow. You got any idea how bad that hurts?"

"I can imagine," I said. "I don't want to find out."

"You're right about that. Behave yourself, and you'll be all right."

"Until I get to *Aeolus*? That it?"

"We're civilized people. We're gonna question you, yeah. But we use drugs. When you wake up, you won't even remember what happened. If you give us the right answers, you may even wake up back in your own bed. Depends."

"How about Mary?"

"It's time to go, Finn. Up the ladder."

I kept my hands out to the sides until I got to the ladder. Then I put one on each handrail and went up the four steps and into the cockpit.

There was a six-inch-square stainless-steel plate on the starboard side of the stern rail that was part of a bracket to hold the dinghy's outboard engine. It was shiny enough to act as a mirror, allowing me to watch Frankie as he came up the ladder. He was using his left hand to hold on, the pistol in his right.

I stood there, swaying with the rolling of the boat. When he mounted the first step, I lost my balance. "Shit!" I barked, catching myself with one hand on each cockpit locker.

Frankie laughed, and that's when I kicked backward with both feet. I caught him in the chest, and he dropped the pistol as he went over backward. The pistol fell in the cockpit, so I left it there.

Twisting, I snatched a winch handle from the holder in the cockpit. I dove down the companionway, landing on Frankie. Knowing his skills as a fighter, I didn't give him a chance. I cracked him on the side of the head with the winch handle. I drew back for a second blow, but he was out cold.

Opening the drawer under the chart table, I grabbed a few cable ties. Rolling him onto his belly, I secured his wrists behind his back. Then I cinched up a tie around his ankles. For good measure, I found a piece of light line and threaded it through the cable ties at his ankles and wrists, drawing them together behind him. He was hogtied, now. When he came to, he was going to be uncomfortable. I retrieved his pistol from the cockpit.

Drawing a glass of water from the galley sink, I tossed it in his face. He sputtered and shook his head, struggling for a few seconds, then going limp.

"Fuck you, Finn. You're a dead man, now."

"I need to ask you a few questions, Frankie. But I don't have any of those nice drugs you were talking about. We'll have to do this the old-fashioned way."

"Like I said, fuck you."

"Frankie, it's only fair for you to know. I've been doing this for a long time. As you said a few minutes ago, it's not my first rodeo. You can answer my questions, and the discomfort you feel now is as bad as it'll get. Or you can be a tough guy. I promise you'll talk, either way. And don't feel the need to impress me. I've seen plenty of tough guys break down over the years."

"Who are you?" he asked.

"We did that already. You know as much about me as you need to. From now on, I'm asking the questions. You're either answering or screaming in pain. Got it?"

"Yeah. What do you want to know?"

"Are you working for O'Hanlon?"

"Yeah."

"Is he here? On *Aeolus*?"

"Yeah."

"Did you kill your parents?"

"No, not me."

"Did O'Hanlon hire somebody?"

"Yeah," he said, drawing it out into a laugh.

"What's funny?"

"You really don't know, do you?"

"Don't try my patience, Frankie."

"Sorry. I figured she told you. Or maybe you were even part of it."

"What did you think she told me?"

"She's a hired killer, Finn. One of the best in the business. I'm not shittin' you, man. Honest."

"You telling me O'Hanlon hired Mary to kill your parents?"

"Yeah. That's the short version."

"I've got plenty of time. Give me the long version. Don't leave anything out."

"They were skimming. I caught them at it, but my uncle knew, anyway."

"Wait. Your uncle?"

"Rory O'Hanlon. He's my mother's brother."

"Jesus," I said. "Nothing like keeping it in the family. You offed your own parents? O'Hanlon had his sister killed?"

"I didn't win any prizes when it came to the parent lottery. They had it coming. Rory felt the same way about them."

"Okay. So O'Hanlon hired her to kill them?"

"Yeah. Not just to kill them. Her real job was to recover the money they'd stolen, and a bunch of files they had. Like business records. He conned them into hiring her to help out in their office, like to spy on them. At least to start with. The other came later."

Everything was falling into place, now. Her whole story was bullshit, except the part about running off with the money and the records. "And did she deliver?"

"She killed them and took off with the money and the records. I caught up with her in Alabama and dragged her sorry ass back to Atlanta. Rory and I were gonna dope her up and question her, but she killed the two men I had guarding her and got away. We've been chasin' her ever since."

I felt the bump against *Carib Princess's* hull right before I heard somebody say, "Hey Frankie?"

He was right under the open port light on the starboard side of the coachroof, from the sound of it. I stuck Frankie's pistol in his mouth and shook my head. He got the message.

"Lie to me and I'll kneecap you. How many?" I asked, my voice soft. "Nod when I get to the right number. One?"

He nodded.

"Make a sound and you'll pay for it in pain," I said, rising to a crouch. I could see the guy's head through the port light.

"Frankie? You ready? I saw the guy come — "

I raised the pistol and shot him, blowing the top of his skull away. I scurried up into the cockpit and picked up a boathook, snagging the RIB before it drifted away. I tied it up and climbed down into it, keeping an eye out for neighbors.

I was in luck. The closest boats were anchored a couple of hundred yards upwind, and I didn't see any signs of life on them. My victim was a slight man, fortunately. I lifted him and rolled him onto *Carib Princess's* side deck.

I climbed up next to him and dragged him to the companionway, lowering him, letting him slide down the ladder. I went below and crouched next to Frankie again.

"Sorry for the interruption. Where were we?"

"I just told you, we been chasin' her ever since she killed my two boys in Atlanta and took off. That's about it."

"So you snatched her off the street in Marin?"

"Yeah. They took her to *Aeolus.* They're waiting for me to bring you back there."

"Okay. Anything else you want to tell me?"

"We can work a trade. You swap me and the files for Mary. I'll get Rory to call it even, and we can all go our separate ways. Just let me make a phone call, and I'll set it up."

I laughed. "I don't think so, Frankie. Not today."

"What other choice do you think you have?"

"I'm going to get Mary. Then she and I will decide where to go from here. See, neither one of us trusts you and O'Hanlon."

"You don't have a chance against the people on *Aeolus*."

"You still don't know who I am, Frankie."

"What do you mean?"

"I mean I've been doing this shit since you were in diapers. I hate to do this, but I'm going to gag you. I know it'll be uncomfortable, but I won't be gone long."

29

I PUT THE DROP BOARDS IN THE COMPANIONWAY AND CLOSED THE sliding hatch, locking it. Frankie or his henchmen cut the padlock I normally used to secure the hatch, but I kept a spare in the cockpit locker.

There was no point in leaving the boat open. I didn't expect visitors, but you could never tell. Until I could dispose of Frankie and his dead friend, I didn't want anybody to find them.

I climbed down into the RIB they used, relieved to see it wasn't marked *Tender to Aeolus* or anything like that. It was 21 feet long; it looked out of place tied alongside *Carib Princess*.

The big RIB wouldn't stand out so much when I approached *Aeolus*. It was a typical tender for a big motor yacht. That was the other reason I decided to use it for my rescue of Mary.

As I approached the marina, I saw that the large yachts were all berthed in the same general area. Not only were there a lot of them, but they were packed together. The only way to see the names would be to ride up and down the fairways between the docks.

My tentative plan was to find *Aeolus* and then tie the RIB to one of the marina's dinghy docks. Depending on the situation aboard *Aeolus*, I would either approach on foot or swim up to her stern platform.

My worries about finding *Aeolus* without being observed were unfounded. I spotted her with no trouble; she was crawling with people in dark, military uniforms. They looked like members of a SWAT team. There were two patrol boats, big gray RIBs with French Douane markings, blocking the fairway.

I changed course and headed for the dingy dock near the marina restaurant. Once I wedged my borrowed RIB in with the others, I strolled back along the boardwalk. When I reached the dock where *Aeolus* was berthed, I found a crowd of gawkers. They were milling around, watching the activity on *Aeolus*. Two policemen in bullet-proof vests were guarding the entrance to the dock.

I joined the crowd, getting myself primed to speak French. Then I overheard two couples speaking American English. They were typical small-boat sailors. I walked up to them, and one of the men gave me a little nod.

"Quite a show," he said.

"Yeah," I said. "What's going on? Drug bust?"

He shook his head. "A multiple murder. Somebody showed up to deliver a truck-load of provisions. Went aboard looking for somebody to accept the order and found five bodies."

Mary worked fast. But then I didn't know how long Frankie and been waiting for me. "Five, huh?" I asked. "Any idea who they were?"

"Nope. Somebody said one was the owner, and the rest were crew."

I thought about it for a few seconds and decided it was a typical enough set of questions for a curious idler like me to ask. "Men? Women? What could have happened?"

"No clue. All men is what we heard."

I shook my head. "Hell of a thing. Might as well be back in Florida, huh?"

"Yeah, no shit," he said.

"Well, I gotta get on with it," I said, sidling away. "Take care."

"Yeah, you too."

Frankie said she was a killer. They knew what she was. How could she have done that? Wouldn't they have been on guard? And where the hell could she be? I was making my way to the taxi stand at the marina entrance, trying to imagine how she'd done it.

My cellphone chimed and vibrated against my thigh. Taking it from my pocket, I entered the unlock code and read the text message. *Glad to see you're back ashore okay. Goodbye for now. Outta here. Ditching this phone. Keep yours, please. Later.*

She must have been watching for me. I felt a pang of sadness, but I could tell from the text that she didn't want my company right now. Resisting the temptation to look for her, I got a taxi to take me to Ste. Anne. I'd make my way back to the boat from there; I could swim if there were no water taxis.

30

CARIB PRINCESS BOBBED AT ANCHOR IN RODNEY BAY'S SLIGHT chop as I approached in the dinghy. I made the three-hour sail from Ste. Anne last night and cleared into St. Lucia first thing this morning.

On my way back to the boat, I stopped at the bakery downstairs from the Port Authority office to pick up pastries and coffee for breakfast. I tied the dinghy alongside and set the paper bag from the bakery on the side deck while I climbed aboard. Settling in the cockpit, I unpacked my food and thought back over the last 24 hours.

I missed Mary. A lot happened since our breakfast ashore in Marin yesterday. I was tired from the stress and the activity, but more than that, I was lonely.

I made my landfall in Rodney Bay, St. Lucia last night after the Port Authority office closed, so I couldn't clear in then. Hungry, I fixed myself a pot of beans and rice with *chorizo*. While it simmered, I stirred in the last packet of Mary's *sazón*.

Wondering where she was, I ate and cleaned up the galley. Then I crashed on the starboard settee. That's where I woke up this morning, half-expecting Mary to bring me coffee. When my head cleared, I gathered up my papers and went ashore to clear into St. Lucia.

I took a bite of *pain au chocolat* and replayed yesterday's events in my mind. The taxi from the marina in Marin dropped me at Ste. Anne's town dock. A water taxi took me back to *Carib Princess* from there.

Everything aboard the boat was as I left it. Frankie gave me a questioning look, but I ignored him. He was of no further use to me.

I opened the drawer where I kept my papers and picked up our passports and the inbound clearance document. With Mary on the run, I needed to leave Martinique myself.

As I took my little inflatable back in to the town dock in Ste. Anne, I thought about how to get Mary off the crew list. The French authorities wouldn't grant me departure clearance unless everyone on the list was accounted for.

Immigration authorities took a dim view of skippers who left crew behind. It was a captain's responsibility to make sure his crew didn't jump ship and stay in the country illegally. I needed to be able to show, on paper at least, that Mary could afford to leave Martinique when her visa expired.

I found a travel agent on a side street in Ste. Anne and made a deal. It cost me a plane ticket back to the States in Mary's name and a couple of hundred euros in gratuities, and I was clear.

The travel agent kept the ticket, and I was sure he would eventually refund the price to his account. But what the hell? He was an authorized agent of French Customs for handling clearance of private conveyances — yachts and aircraft. That meant he could handle my outbound clearance to St. Lucia, which was an unexpected benefit.

Back aboard *Carib Princess*, I packed up the dinghy and got under way. Once I was in deep water out in the St. Lucia Channel, I hove to long enough to say goodbye to Frankie and his friend. A few feet of anchor chain around their ankles would keep them out of sight permanently.

So here I sat in Rodney Bay, single again, and more than a little depressed. Struggling not to read more than I should into Mary's brief text from yesterday, I thought about how she escaped after she wasted O'Hanlon and his boys. She was one hell of a woman, Mary was.

I made myself take her text at face value. She saw me come ashore, so she must have been in the marina somewhere. Ignoring a wave of regret at having failed to see her, I wondered if she had waited to see if I tried to come to her rescue. I would let myself believe that. What was the harm?

She made short work of O'Hanlon and his pals. Though I was sad that she opted to run instead of making her way back to *Carib Princess*, I understood her decision.

Frankie said she was a pro; he was right. She cleaned out O'Hanlon and his pals and got clear. She needed to distance herself from her immediate past. That's exactly what I would have done in her situation.

She must have had another passport stashed in Martinique. Or she found her own means of getting one. *What about money, though?* Then I realized she probably ripped off O'Hanlon again. He no doubt kept a good bit of money close at hand. People like him were never without plenty of cash. Besides, she was carrying her purse when his goons snatched her. She would have recovered it before she left *Aeolus*.

I thought about that purse. It was in her backpack when she first joined me. When she was away from the backpack, she always carried the purse. It was nothing fancy. Like her other belongings, it was utilitarian.

When I checked through her things early on, I skipped the purse. I was looking for weapons or drugs, not personal stuff. The purse wasn't big enough to conceal anything that would have worried me back then. But she could have kept another identity tucked away in the lining. Maybe that's how she did it.

Thinking of her passport reminded me that I should add her new one to the stash that was fiberglassed into the keel. Mary Helen Maloney, Mary Elizabeth O'Brien. That brought to mind her quip about the foreign-born Irish. I felt a smile spreading over my face, the first one since we parted.

I was feeling lucky. Fate brought us together the first time. Maybe my luck would hold.

Meanwhile, I was overdue checking my satellite phone. I skipped it last night. Unlocking the companionway, I ducked below and retrieved it.

Back in the cockpit, I took another pastry out of the bag while the phone acquired a satellite connection. I took a bite and washed it down with some coffee before the phone pinged.

My employer was looking for me. I entered the security code and opened the text.

Ready for another project?

I grinned. Work would keep me from pining away for Mary, if nothing else. Who knew when I would see her again? Maybe never, given what we both did for a living.

Yes. When and where?

St. Thomas. Earliest convenience. Encrypted email to confirm details within 12 hours.

I keyed in *Okay. Thanks.*

I finished my breakfast and coffee. St. Thomas was a three-day sail. It was also part of the U.S. That was unusual. The target must be a foreign national. Would they want me to carry this out on U.S. soil? Probably not, but it wasn't unheard of.

If there were constraints, they would be spelled out in the email. Until I knew more, I would rest. There would be time enough to make plans when I got the email. For now, I would rig my big awning to shade the boat. Then I would sling my hammock and laze the day away.

EPILOGUE

Once again, I was the first one in the door when the Port Authority office opened the next morning. The same agent who cleared me in yesterday handled my outbound clearance.

"You don' stay long in our beautiful country, captain. Every-t'ing good, I hope?"

"Yes, thanks," I said. "Everything's fine. I just have to meet somebody in St. Thomas a little earlier than I thought. Don't worry; I'll be back. St. Lucia's always a great place to visit."

"We try to make it be that way. You are kind to say so. God bless, and have a safe voyage. Come back soon, captain."

She stamped my papers and handed them to me across the desk.

"Thank you, ma'am," I said. "Stay well."

She smiled and nodded as I stood up and left. I headed downstairs to the bakery and bought pastries and coffee for another breakfast in the cockpit.

Back aboard, I took a sip of coffee and thought about the follow-up email from my client that came last night. The target was a known member of ISIS. He was also a U.S. citizen, native born. They've been looking for this character for a couple of years. He was recently picked up through face ID when he entered the U.S. in St. Thomas.

I finished my pastry and took a last swallow of coffee. I was ready to go; there was no point in lingering. I had a three-day sail ahead of me. There would be plenty of time to think about my new mission. And about Mary, and the time we enjoyed together.

I was busy getting the boat ready for sea when I was interrupted by an incoming text on my smartphone. I entered my unlock code and glanced at the originating number. The message was from the 904 area code in the U.S. That was north Florida. I didn't know anybody in north Florida.

I opened the message and read:

Happy to see you got along all right with Frankie, but I knew you would. Don't bother looking for me. I left the area once I spotted you on the dock. I'm touched that you came to help, but not surprised. I could tell you feel the same way I do about us.

I'm on my way back to where I came from. Got a couple more people to see back home before I can rest. Just ditch the stuff I left behind, please. I'm going to be honing my acting skills for a while until this quiets down.

Sorry to run, but one of these days soon, I'll be in touch. Keep your phone number so I can reach you. I'm ditching this one as soon as I hit send. I'll let you know when I get one you can use to reach me.

I'm thinking we could start over from the same place, maybe in a month or so, but I'll let you know as the time gets closer.

I miss you, but it won't be long until I see you again. You were right; we make a good team. And just in case you couldn't tell, I love you.

Mary Beth

.   .   .

THE PLACE we started wasn't too far from where I was headed now. Going to St. Thomas would give me a chance to change the boat's name again. I would clear her in there as *Carib Princess.* When she left there wouldn't be any outbound clearance required, since she was U.S. flagged.

Once under way, I would heave to and change her name back to *Island Girl.* I was partial to that name. While Mary Beth was around, I thought of *her* as my island girl. I grinned at the thought that she would be again, and soon.

THE END

MAILING LIST

THANK YOU FOR READING *ASSASSINS AND LIARS*.

SIGN up for my mailing list at http://eepurl.com/bKujyv for notice of new releases and special sales or giveaways. I'll email a link to you for a free download of my short story, **The Lost Tourist Franchise**, when you sign up. I promise not to use the list for anything else; I dislike spam as much as you do.

A NOTE TO THE READER

Thank you again for reading *Assassins and Liars*, the first book in the **J.R. Finn Sailing Mystery Series.** I hope you enjoyed it. If so, please leave a brief review on Amazon.

Reviews are of great benefit to independent authors like me; they help me more than you can imagine. They are a primary means to help new readers find my work. A few words from you can help others find the pleasure that I hope you found in this book, as well as keeping my spirits up as I work on the next one.

In September 2020, I published *Sharks and Prey*, the eighth novel in the **J.R. Finn Sailing Mystery** series. The latest book in the series is due to be published in August, 2021. This series is also available in audiobook format.

———

I also write two other sailing-thriller series set in the Caribbean. If you enjoyed the adventures of Finn and Mary, you'll enjoy the **Bluewater Thrillers** and the **Connie Barrera Thrillers.**

The **Bluewater Thrillers** feature two young women, Dani Berger and Liz Chirac. Dani and Liz sail a luxury charter yacht named *Vengeance*. They often find trouble, but they can take care of themselves.

The **Connie Barrera Thrillers** are a spin-off from the **Bluewater Thrillers**. Before Connie went to sea, she was a first-rate con artist. Dani and Liz met Connie in *Bluewater Ice*, and they taught her to sail. She liked it so much she bought a charter yacht of her own.

Dani and Liz also introduced her to Paul Russo, a retired Miami homicide detective. Paul signed on as her first mate and chef, but he ended up as her husband. Connie and Paul run a charter sailing yacht named *Diamantista*. Like Dani and Liz, they're often beset by problems unrelated to sailing.

The **Bluewater Thrillers** and the **Connie Barrera Thrillers** share many of the same characters. Phillip Davis and his wife Sandrine, Sharktooth, and Marie LaCroix often appear in both series, as do Connie, Paul, Dani, and Liz. Here's a link to the web page that lists those novels in order of publication: http://www.clrdougherty.com/p/bluewater-thrillers-and-connie-barrera.html

———

A list of all my books is on the last page; just click on a title or go to my website for more information.

If you'd like to know when my next book is released, visit my author's page on Amazon at www.amazon.com/author/clrdougherty and click the "Follow" link or sign up for my mailing list at http://eepurl.com/bKujyv for information on sales and special promotions. I welcome email correspondence about books, boats and sailing. My address is clrd@clrdougherty.com. I enjoy hearing from people who read my books; I

always answer email from readers. Thanks again for your
support.

ABOUT THE AUTHOR

Welcome aboard!

Charles Dougherty is a lifelong sailor; he's lived what he writes. He and his wife have spent over 30 years sailing together.

For 15 years, they lived aboard their boat full-time, cruising the East Coast and the Caribbean islands. They spent most of that time exploring the Eastern Caribbean.

Dougherty is well acquainted with the islands and their people. The characters and locations in his novels reflect his experience.

A storyteller before all else, Dougherty lets his characters speak for themselves. Pick up one of his thrillers and listen to the sound of adventure as you smell the salt air. Enjoy the views of distant horizons and meet some people you won't forget.

Dougherty's sailing fiction books include the **Bluewater Thrillers**, the **Connie Barrera Thrillers**, and the **J.R. Finn Sailing Mysteries.**

Dougherty's first novel was *Deception in Savannah*. While it's not about sailing, one of the main characters is Connie Barrera. He had so much fun with Connie that he built a sailing series around her.

Before writing Connie's series, he wrote the first three Bluewater Thrillers, about two young women running a charter yacht in the islands. In the fourth book, Connie shows up as their charter guest.

She stayed for the fifth Bluewater book. Then Connie demanded her own series.

The J.R. Finn books are his newest sailing series. The first Finn book, though it begins in Puerto Rico, starts with a real-life encounter that Dougherty had in St. Lucia. For more information about that, visit his website.

Dougherty's other fiction works are the *Redemption of Becky Jones*, a psycho-thriller, and *The Lost Tourist Franchise*, a short story about another of the characters from Deception in Savannah.

Dougherty has also written two non-fiction books. *Life's a Ditch* is the story of how he and his wife moved aboard their sailboat, Play Actor, and their adventures along the east coast of the U.S. *Dungda de Islan'* relates their experiences while cruising the Caribbean.

Charles Dougherty welcomes email correspondence with readers.

www.clrdougherty.com
clrd@clrdougherty.com

OTHER BOOKS BY C.L.R. DOUGHERTY

Bluewater Thrillers

Bluewater Killer

Bluewater Vengeance

Bluewater Voodoo

Bluewater Ice

Bluewater Betrayal

Bluewater Stalker

Bluewater Bullion

Bluewater Rendezvous

Bluewater Ganja

Bluewater Jailbird

Bluewater Drone

Bluewater Revolution

Bluewater Enigma

Bluewater Quest

Bluewater Target

Bluewater Blackmail

Bluewater Clickbait

Bluewater Thrillers Boxed Set: Books 1-3

Connie Barrera Thrillers

From Deception to Betrayal - An Introduction to Connie Barrera

Love for Sail - A Connie Barrera Thriller

Sailor's Delight - A Connie Barrera Thriller

A Blast to Sail - A Connie Barrera Thriller

Storm Sail - A Connie Barrera Thriller

Running Under Sail - A Connie Barrera Thriller

Sails Job - A Connie Barrera Thriller

Under Full Sail - A Connie Barrera Thriller

An Easy Sail - A Connie Barrera Thriller

A Torn Sail - A Connie Barrera Thriller

A Righteous Sail - A Connie Barrera Thriller

Sailor Take Warning - A Connie Barrera Thriller

Sailor's Choice - A Connie Barrera Thriller

J.R. Finn Sailing Mysteries

Assassins and Liars

Avengers and Rogues

Vigilantes and Lovers

Sailors and Sirens

Villains and Vixens

Killers and Keepers

Devils and Divas

Sharks and Prey

Other Fiction

Deception in Savannah

The Redemption of Becky Jones

The Lost Tourist Franchise

Books for Sailors and Dreamers

Life's a Ditch

Dungda de Islan'

Audiobooks

Assassins and Liars

Avengers and Rogues

Vigilantes and Lovers

Sailors and Sirens

Villains and Vixens

Killers and Keepers

Devils and Divas

Sharks and Prey

For more information please visit www.clrdougherty.com

Or visit www.amazon.com/author/clrdougherty

Made in the USA
Middletown, DE
08 February 2022

60775893R00106